Desert Devil

Desert Devil

Rena McKay

THORNDIKE
CHIVERS

This Large Print edition is published by Thorndike Press®, Waterville, Maine USA and by BBC Audiobooks, Ltd, Bath, England.

Published in 2004 in the U.S. by arrangement with Maureen Moran Agency.

Published in 2004 in the U.K. by arrangement with the author.

U.S. Hardcover 0-7862-6567-1 (Romance)
U.K. Hardcover 0-7540-9645-9 (Chivers Large Print)

The text of this Large Print edition is unabridged.
Other aspects of the book may vary from the original edition.

Set in 16 pt. Plantin by Ramona Watson.

Printed in the United States on permanent paper.

British Library Cataloguing-in-Publication Data available

Library of Congress Cataloging-in-Publication Data

McKay, Rena.
    Desert devil / Rena McKay.
        p. cm.
    ISBN 0-7862-6567-1 (lg. print : hc : alk. paper)
    1. Business intelligence — Fiction.   2. Inventions —
Fiction.   3. Arizona — Fiction.   4. Large type books.
I. Title.
PS3563.C3449D47 2004
    813'.6—dc22   2004045991

Desert Devil

Chapter One

Juli Townsend's little car shuddered as another of the big trucks roared by on the narrow, two-lane highway. She gripped the steering wheel with the unhappy feeling that at any moment she might find herself impaled on one of the thorny cactus plants crowding in on the dark ribbon of highway. She caught a brief glimpse of the name TAYLOR ELECTRONICS emblazoned on the side of the trailer, and she made an angry mental note to tell Mr. T. J. Taylor exactly what she thought of his truck drivers when she saw him. Among a few other things she intended to tell him, she thought determinedly.

The road topped a small rise and then the town of Cholla, Arizona, was spread out below her, looking somehow insignificant surrounded by the sprawling, barren miles of flat desert and the jagged blue silhouette of mountains in the far distance. At the edge of the road was a large green sign announcing that Cholla was the home of Taylor Electronics, plus a brief statement proclaiming that the company was bringing jobs, progress, and prosperity to the area. A large map showed the way through town to the company grounds, though that was hardly necessary since the bulky, tan-colored buildings dominated the northeastern section of the small town.

The town was quite distinctly divided into two areas, Juli noted as the car descended the gradual incline and crossed a bridge over a totally dry riverbed. The old section looked a little dilapidated, with faded stucco buildings and straggling fences, but the streets were pleasantly shaded with cottonwoods and an occasional palm tree. The new section had a bustling shopping center and row after row of bare, new-looking houses on streets that simply plunged out into the desert and stopped abruptly among the dry shrubs and cactus.

Juli glanced at her watch. Almost twelve o'clock. She had intended to arrive in Cholla in time to locate David's trailer and freshen up before keeping her one o'clock appointment with Mr. Taylor, but a broken fan belt on the car's engine had delayed her. Now she decided she would simply grab a bite of lunch and go directly to the appointment. She'd had several days on the road in which to decide exactly what she wanted to say to Mr. Taylor, and she thought she had it all letter-perfect by now. She would be courteous, but firm. Tactful, but resolute. Reasonable, but shrewd.

And if that didn't work, she thought grimly, she would simply accuse Mr. T. J. Taylor of cheating and theft and tell him David's mother intended to sue for every cent the company was worth.

She stopped at a small but clean little Spanish-style restaurant in the older section of town and had a deliciously spicy cheese enchilada and green salad for lunch. She inquired about directions to Reynaldo Road, where David's trailer was located, and decided she should have no trouble finding it later. After lunch she freshened her light makeup in the ladies' room, and a few minutes later confidently parked her car in Taylor Electronics' spacious parking lot.

Up close the tan-colored buildings looked even larger and bulkier than they had from a distance. A discreet sign pointed to the office, a smaller two-story, tile-roofed building set off by itself. It was tastefully landscaped with red cinder rock and a variety of desert plants. Everything looked almost scrupulously neat, Juli noted. No noisy machinery, no billows of smoke polluting the cloudless desert sky.

The midday February sunshine actually felt hot on Juli's back as she crossed the parking lot. She marveled to think that only a few days ago she had been sloshing through ice and snow back in Ohio. She opened the heavy glass door and walked up to the reception desk. A dark-haired young woman rose to meet her.

Juli gave her name. "I have a one o'clock appointment with Mr. Taylor," she added.

The girl checked a calendar on her desk. "Yes. Would you come this way, please?"

She indicated a low swinging door at the end of the desk, and Juli followed her through the rows of desks and across the large room. The room was not noisy, and yet it had the steady hum of busy typewriters, low voices, and whirring office machinery that indicated an efficient, smoothly running organization. The girl stopped at a closed door marked CONFERENCE ROOM, opened it, and stood aside to let Juli enter.

"Mr. Taylor will be a few minutes late. His noon meeting ran overtime. Would you care for a cup of coffee while you're waiting?"

Julie started to decline, felt her palms

suddenly dampen with nervous perspiration, and nodded affirmatively, instead. The girl said she would return with a cup in a minute.

Juli paced restlessly around the room trying to quell this sudden explosion of nervousness. Her soft brown hair clung damply to her temples, and her white shell blouse and coral slacks suddenly felt wrinkled and too casual for this businesslike atmosphere. But there was nothing to be nervous about, she reminded herself firmly. She had only to point out to Mr. Taylor that she and her aunt were well aware of the valuable contribution David had made to the company and only wanted what was rightfully his.

But somehow Juli had not expected an electronics company set out in the middle of the Arizona desert to be quite so intimidating. She had vaguely pictured her cousin David performing his experiments or inventing his strange contraptions in the dusty backroom of some little shop, not working for what was obviously an extremely up-to-date, progressive organization. And yet she knew that vague thought was illogical, of course. Dusty little shops didn't hire brilliant university graduates to run a complete research department.

And a mere insurance secretary didn't usually have the temerity to demand a conference with a company president, either, she suddenly thought shakily.

The girl returned with coffee and packets of powdered cream and sugar. She assured Juli that Mr. Taylor would be with her as soon as possible. Juli thanked her and perched on the edge of a russet-colored sofa to sip her coffee. A real leather sofa, she noted as she ran a finger lightly over the glove-soft surface. Taylor Electronics obviously did not go in for cheap imitations. No doubt they could afford the best, she reminded herself grimly, if they were in the habit of cheating their employees, as David's last letter had certainly seemed to indicate.

Coffee cup in hand, she rose and wandered around the room again. With the comfortable sofa, several easy chairs, lamps, and a big coffee table, the room looked more like a living room than a formal conference room. The window looked out on a small, louver-enclosed area of green vines and shrubs. Turning restlessly, she walked toward a far wall on which hung several enlarged color prints of what was evidently the Taylor Electronics plant when it was under construction. An artist's conception of the completed project showed the company evidently planned further expansion sometime in the future. Then her attention was drawn to a framed photograph of a distinguished-looking, silvery-haired man. A small brass plaque on the frame identified him as Thomas J. Taylor.

Julie inspected the photograph and suddenly felt reassured. Thomas J. Taylor looked competent and businesslike, but certainly neither unkind nor dishonest. There was a hint of good humor in the crinkled lines around his eyes and mouth. He surely wouldn't be unfeeling about the problems of a crippled widow, dependent primarily on her only son for support, Juli decided. She mentally revised her plans to include a greater appeal to his sympathies.

Juli heard the door open and she turned expectantly. But the tall man whose broad shoulders filled the doorway was not the silvery-haired gentleman she had expected to see. This man appeared to be in his early thirties. His thick brown hair had a glint of bronze, and his lean, handsome face was deeply tanned. He wore a well-cut gray suit and gave a general impression of rugged elegance. One tanned hand carried a manila file folder. As he closed the door and strode toward her, Juli had the uneasy impression his remote gray-green eyes held a hint of contemptuous mockery. There was nothing but expressionless cool courtesy in his voice when he spoke, however.

"Miss Townsend?"

Juli's momentary feeling of reassurance evaporated like a drop of water sizzling under desert sun. This man's manner was one of steely reserve, and Juli knew instantly that an appeal to his sympathies would be useless. She had the unnerving feeling that his appraising look boldly traveling over her classified her as attractive and then dismissed that fact as immaterial to the business at hand. He sat lightly on the arm of an easy chair and flicked open the file folder with a well-shaped hand.

"I have your letter here —" he began.

His voice held a hint of the same contempt his eyes had revealed, and Juli's nervousness suddenly changed to anger. She had made an appointment with the president of the company, and she did not intend to discuss this matter with anyone but the president himself. Certainly not with this man, whose coolly superior manner she found both infuriating and intimidating. She set her coffee cup down and straightened her shoulders.

"I'd rather wait and talk to Mr. Taylor

14

personally," she said, matching his coolness as her blue eyes lifted to meet his gray-green ones defiantly.

He lifted a dark eyebrow. "I *am* Mr. Taylor."

"You are? But I thought —" The dismayed words popped out before Juli could stop them, and her glance flew to the portrait of the silvery-haired gentleman.

His glance followed hers. "My father," he said briefly, "founder of the company. He died of a heart attack about six years ago, just after we moved the plant out here from Phoenix. I am Thorne Taylor, president of Taylor Electronics."

Thorne Taylor. The T. J. Taylor of her letter, who was definitely not the stern but kindly looking gentleman in the photograph. "I'm sorry," Juli began, flustered. "I didn't know —"

"Sorry about my father's death? Or sorry to find that *I* am company president?"

His mocking voice taunted her, flustering her even further. She twisted the strap of her purse nervously and looked away from those disturbing gray-green eyes as she struggled to regain her composure. Why was he doing this? she wondered angrily. Somehow he had managed to put her on the defensive with that unexpected and totally uncalled-for remark. Which was probably exactly what he intended to do, she realized. No wonder David had been so suspicious of him.

Juli took a deep breath. "I'm sorry about your father, of course." Struggling to reverse their positions and put him on the defensive, she added, "It must have been very difficult for you taking over the responsibilities and management of the company when you were so young." She managed to inject a slightly condescending note into her voice, as if she could forgive his behavior because of his youth. A moment later she regretted her remark.

"I don't think you are in any position to make disparaging remarks about *youth*," he said softly as he leaned toward her slightly, his eyes taking in her fair skin and shoulder length, wavy brown hair, which she had long since despaired of ever looking sleek and sophisticated.

"I'm twenty-two!" Juli flared. Then she bit her lip, angry that she was on the defensive again, shouting out her age like some pouting child. She took another deep, shaky breath. This wasn't going the way she had planned at all. She started again. "I made this appointment with you because I am representing my aunt, Katherine Flynn. Her son, David Flynn, was employed by Taylor Electronics until his death a little over two months ago."

Thorne Taylor just sat there eyeing her reflectively, waiting for her to go on. He obviously did not intend to say or do anything to make this interview any easier for her.

"David had been working for you for several years, I believe —"

"Two," he cut in.

Juli ignored the interruption. "David, as head of your research department —"

"David Flynn was not head of the research department at Taylor Electronics," Thorne Taylor said flatly. "That position belongs to Dr. Richard Johnson, who has held it for almost five years."

Juli looked at him with a mixture of doubt and dismay. She was sure Aunt Kate had said David was head of the department. But she must have been mistaken. She tried to keep the discrepancy from disrupting what she wanted to say.

"I'm sure you'll recall that David had a brilliant university record. He also held patents on some improvements he had made in the electronics field." Under Thorne Taylor's steady gaze, Juli's voice wavered lamely. "Some . . . some tubes or something, I think it was."

17

Thorne Taylor flipped the file open again. Looking at the top page upside down, Juli recognized the last letter she had written requesting this appointment. His head was down as he studied the letter. His eyelashes, she noted irrelevantly, were the same color as his hair, rich brown glinted with bronze.

"Just what is it you are getting at, Miss Townsend?" Thorne Taylor asked abruptly, his voice almost dangerously polite. He glanced up sharply, catching Juli studying him, and she felt a tinge of pink warm her cheeks.

For a moment the impact of those gray-green eyes sent her carefully planned speech spinning. She clutched at it wildly. "I just wanted — what I mean is —" She swallowed convulsively and concentrated her gaze on the safety of the walnut paneling on the opposite wall. "My aunt and I happen to know that shortly before his death, David had just discovered or . . . or invented something of considerable value to the company. He seemed to think —" Juli hesitated, disliking the tentative sound of that. More firmly, she added, "He was certain his invention would be worth a great deal of money. In fact, he was already planning to bring his mother out here to live. Since he is now dead, it would seem only fair that his mother be awarded whatever monetary considerations were involved."

"I see."

Out of the corner of her eyes she saw his head tilt to study the file, and she dared to look at him again. His build, though powerful, was lean and trim, without an ounce of excess fat. He had fine lines radiating from the corners of his eyes like his father, but his had the look of the outdoorsman accustomed to gazing over wide expanses of desert space. This would have been much easier, she thought unhappily, if she really could have talked to the stern but kindly looking elder Mr. Taylor.

"Miss Townsend," Thorne Taylor began, closing the file again, "you should be aware that anything David 'discovered or invented' on company time belongs to the company. I'm sure we have a signed agreement to that effect."

Juli bit her lip. She had wondered about that, too, of course, but David's final letter had been so emphatic in saying that Taylor wouldn't be able to cheat him this time. "I believe David had done something to protect his interests," she finally said hesitantly. "And his mother's," she added.

Thorne Taylor leaned over and pressed a button on the wall. A moment later a tawny-haired young woman about Juli's age appeared carrying a steno notebook.

"Would you get David Flynn's personnel folder for me, please?" he requested. "It is probably in the inactive file by now."

The young woman nodded, her eyes darting curiously to Juli, then returning to Thorne. There was something oddly melting about the way she looked at him, and with sudden intuition Juli suspected the young woman's feelings for her boss were not strictly secretarial. Which wasn't surprising, Juli thought grudgingly. He was attractive. More than attractive, she thought even more reluctantly. He had a certain raw masculinity, a primitive virility that seemed only thinly veiled by the business suit and well-groomed hands and hair. There was a strength and litheness to his movements that suggested power held under taut control, an intensity in those gray-green eyes that hinted at fiery depths of passion under different circumstances.

And that was certainly a strange turn for her thoughts to be taking, Juli thought shakily, suddenly horrified with herself. She had come here to see that justice was done to her Aunt Kate, not to react like some star-struck adolescent to the first attractive man she met, particularly a man whose attraction was so purely and blatantly physical.

"This may take a few minutes," Thorne Taylor said. Dryly, he added, "We keep most of our records on computer, of course. But I presume you'll want to see our agreement with your cousin in his own handwriting."

Juli nodded stiffly.

While they waited for the young woman to return with the personnel file, Thorne Taylor regarded her reflectively. Finally, he asked, "Are you planning to be in Cholla long?"

"Just long enough to pack up David's personal things to take back to his mother, plus arrange to sell his trailer and property here. And get this matter with your company straightened out," she added firmly.

He failed to show any reaction to that comment. "What do you do back in —" He paused, checked the file again. "Back in Ohio?"

"I'm a secretary in the national offices of an insurance company located in our town," she replied.

"On vacation?" he inquired politely.

"My boss was kind enough to give me a

leave of absence to take care of these matters for David's mother. She had a stroke a while back and is partially paralyzed on one side."

"How unfortunate." His voice, though unemotional, did sound faintly regretful, and Juli gave him a hopeful sidelong glance.

"You're alone, then?" he added casually.

For a moment Juli wondered if he could have some personal reason for asking that question. Then she scoffed at herself. She was reading too much into a polite inquiry. Thorne Taylor certainly had no *personal* interest in whether or not she was alone.

"Yes, I'm alone. David's mother is unable to travel at present. She has been taking physical therapy treatments and I believe she's improving. Everyone thought she should go to a nursing home, but she's always refused, and somehow she's managed on her own." Juli hesitated. "David was providing most of her financial support. That's why I think she's entitled to whatever David had coming to him."

He nodded, sending Juli's hopes spiraling upward. "I'm sure that's true," he agreed. Then his voice hardened and the gray-green eyes turned steely. "However, so far as I know, David had nothing coming above and beyond his regular salary."

"But his letter said —" Juli broke off, trying to remember David's exact wording. The letter was in her purse and she longed to snatch it out, but she restrained herself. She had decided before coming here that if Taylor Electronics proved balky that the letter might best be saved for showing to an attorney. "David wrote that he definitely had made an important scientific discovery — a 'breakthrough,' I believe he called it."

Just then the young woman returned with the personnel folder. She waited a moment, looking hopeful, but Thorne Taylor dismissed her with a brief nod. He extracted a page from the folder and handed it to Juli. It was, as he had indicated, what appeared to be a completely legal agreement signifying that anything David produced while employed in the research department of Taylor Electronics belonged to the company.

"It's standard procedure," he said briefly. "The company can hardly afford to run a research department for the private benefit of its researchers, although we do have a fairly generous incentive and bonus program for outstanding achievements."

Juli handed the sheet back, feeling

slightly bewildered, her eyes not meeting his. Then she remembered another of the arguments she had mustered in case something like this came up. "But I believe there was a well-publicized court case not long ago in which a man was awarded a substantial amount of money from a company which had earlier paid him only a very small sum for an invention he produced while he was working for them."

Thorne Taylor gave her a long, thoughtful look, as if perhaps reassessing her. "You're considering a court case?" he inquired.

Juli lifted her head defiantly. "If necessary," she stated.

But if she thought she had won any victory or pressured him into any concessions, she was wrong.

"Your information about a previous court case may very well be accurate," he agreed coolly. "But a specific invention of proven worth was involved. Just what did David produce that you are trying to tell me is so valuable?"

Juli looked at him in dismay, then glanced away quickly before those gray-green eyes could entrap her. She had been so sure that once she confronted the company with her "knowledge" of David's valuable invention or discovery, they could hardly deny its existence. And yet that appeared to be exactly what Thorne Taylor was doing. He was challenging her to prove David had made some important contribution, to identify his invention — a challenge she was afraid he knew she was unprepared to meet.

Damn David and his secretiveness! she suddenly thought with irrational anger. Why hadn't he explained to his mother what he had invented so they wouldn't be in this awkward position? Why had he been so slyly mysterious? And then she sighed inwardly, guiltily. David probably wasn't being intentionally mysterious or secretive. He had undoubtedly thought that even if he did explain, neither his mother nor Juli had sufficient scientific knowledge or training to understand. And, of course, he certainly hadn't expected to meet his death in a car accident so soon afterward.

Finally, Juli said aloofly, "I imagine, if the case should go to court, that your own company records would reveal David's accomplishments — providing the records are not tampered with, of course."

That statement brought Thorne Taylor to his feet, his face dark with anger, and for one panicky moment Juli thought she had gone too far. His chiseled lips compressed into a thin line, and a muscle jerked along his lean jaw. Juli drew back, blue eyes wide, again aware of that raw, almost primitive masculinity about him that seemed intensified by the surge of anger. She suddenly reached for the coffee cup and took a shaky sip of the now-cold liquid, her eyes meeting his warily over the rim, as if the cup were somehow a protective barrier between them.

With what was evidently a supreme effort at self-control, he relaxed his clenched hands. "Tell me, Miss Townsend, how well did you know your cousin David?"

The question caught Juli by surprise. She toyed with the cup in her hands, uncertain how to answer. In one way, she thought she knew David very well. In another, she wasn't sure she knew him at all. Her mother and David's mother were sisters, and the two families were close when Juli was growing up. David had always been her good friend, even though he was eight years older. She loved the crazy inventions he was always bringing around to show her. Silly contraptions where the pull of a string or push of a switch would set into motion a whole series of wildly

26

moving parts that would then result in the accomplishment of some mundane little task, like squeezing a tube of toothpaste or stamping a letter. He amused her with silly jokes and taught her little "magic" tricks.

He won awards in high school, and Juli proudly reported to her grade-school friends that he was the smartest boy in the whole world. But one time one of those friends scornfully retorted that her older sister had dated him and he was "weird." Juli had practically flown at her, demanding that the girl take that back, but she wouldn't, even adding that David was "funny looking" and "crazy."

Juli had frigidly dropped the girl from among her circle of friends, and no one else ever dared say anything about David — at least not *to* Juli, though sometimes she had the unhappy feeling they giggled about him behind her back. Even back then, she supposed, she had realized he was different from the usual run of high school boys. He was a loner, awkward at sports and dancing, a very complex person. But he wasn't "funny looking" or "crazy" just because he was plump and wore bottle-thick glasses and was too smart for most people to understand, she sometimes thought with fierce protectiveness.

And even those little quirks seemed to straighten out when he went off to college on a scholarship. He switched to contact lenses, lost weight, and learned to get along better socially. Unfortunately, Juli more or less lost contact with him about that time, except for what she heard through Aunt Kate. Juli had her own problems then, of course: her mother's painful illness and unexpected death; the months of numbed loss; her father's surprising remarriage to a younger woman with three small children.

She did know, through Aunt Kate, that things didn't go as well for David after college graduation as everyone had expected. Somehow he just hadn't seemed to live up to the earlier promise he had shown. He changed jobs frequently, complaining that the companies he worked for were too rigid, that he didn't have enough creative freedom. He seemed generous with financial help for his mother, though Juli sometimes suspected that the money came less regularly than Aunt Kate let on. Aunt Kate had been so excited when she got his letter about the "scientific breakthrough" and his promise that he would soon have the money to bring her out to live in Arizona.

And then came the shocking call about

his death in a car accident. . . . Juli took a deep, shuddering breath.

"Are you all right?" Thorne Taylor demanded sharply, peering down at her with a sort of suspicious concern.

"Yes, I . . . I'm all right. I was just thinking about David. I still find it hard to believe he's dead."

"You didn't answer my question," he prompted.

"I think I knew him fairly well," she finally said cautiously. She realized the paper cup was beginning to crumple under her nervous handling. She set it aside and tried to keep her hands confidently motionless. "Well enough to know that he was certainly capable of producing something of commercial value in the electronics field."

"I won't argue with that. That was the reason we hired him," Thorne Taylor agreed. Harshly, he added, "The question is, what, if anything, did he produce?"

Juli had the unpleasant feeling this conversation was simply going in circles, getting nowhere. The arguments which had sounded so persuasive when she planned them earlier now seemed as flimsy and leaky as a sieve.

Thorne Taylor suddenly seemed to come

to the same conclusion. He picked up the folders where he had set them on the coffee table and tapped them impatiently against his other hand. With dismay, Juli suddenly realized the discussion was about to be terminated, and she had accomplished nothing at all.

"Mr. Taylor, you must realize that if you refuse to . . . to make any financial settlement, my aunt is fully prepared to take this matter to court!" she exclaimed, the words coming out more breathlessly than she intended.

"Indeed," he murmured. He tilted a dark eyebrow. "Is this a warning that is supposed to frighten me into going along with your cheap little trick to bluff some sort of payment out of my company?"

"Cheap — little — trick!" Juli repeated with incredulous fury, so angry the words were hardly coherent. She struggled for control. "Mr. Taylor, I . . . I assure you that though *you* may have cheated David in the past, I am not going to let you get away with cheating his mother!"

Thorne Taylor's eyes narrowed dangerously. "I wouldn't be tossing around wild, unsubstantiated accusations if I were you," he growled.

Julie tore open her purse and jerked out

David's incriminating letter. She thrust it at him, her breath coming in short gasps, as if she had been running at full speed. "Perhaps you won't think my accusations are so wild when you read this!"

He accepted the wrinkled letter, his eyes holding hers until he dropped his gaze to the scrawled writing.

"The first part is just personal to his mother," Juli said hastily. She turned the page over in his hand. "It's in the last paragraph."

She watched him skim over the scribbled lines quickly, then go back and read them again more slowly. "Is that all you have?" he finally said disdainfully.

"All!" Juli gasped. "It says he has made this scientific breakthrough on something he's been working on for a long time, something he doubted had ever been approached really scientifically before. It says he'll soon have enough money to bring Aunt Kate out to live with him. And it says that *you*, Mr. Taylor, will not be able to cheat him out of anything *this* time!"

Thorne Taylor's broad shoulders moved in a careless shrug, which only angered Juli more. And with increased fury she realized he had tricked her into showing him her one piece of evidence.

"I wondered when I received your letter just what sort of con game you were going to try to pull. Now I know," he said contemptuously. One hand suddenly shot out and caught her shoulder in a cruel grip, the strong fingers biting so harshly into the soft flesh that she stifled a gasp. His eyes burned into hers. "I can tell you're an amateur at the con-game business, Miss Townsend. I suggest you get out of it before the going gets a little rough."

Juli's breath caught as she looked up into that hard, unrelenting face, too stunned and angry even to object to the painful grip on her shoulder. "How . . . how dare you accuse me!" she finally managed to gasp.

The grip loosened, leaving pale, bloodless marks where his fingers had crushed her skin. Instinctively, she rubbed the sore area with her other hand.

"Enjoy your stay in Cholla," he said with a derisive smile and an exaggeratedly polite nod of his head. "You've come at our most pleasant time of year."

Juli watched in furious astonishment as the door closed behind his broad shoulders, trying to comprehend what had just happened. Not only had Thorne Taylor rejected any claim of Aunt Kate's to payments for David's invention; he had denied any such invention even existed. And he had contemptuously accused Juli herself of trying to pull some tricky "con game" on the company!

Or was that, she thought suddenly, just a cheap trick to try to frighten her? David's letter plainly indicated Thorne Taylor was not to be trusted. And he seemed exactly the kind of man who would believe the best form of defense was attack.

Juli jammed the letter back in her purse and snapped the catch shut with a savage twist. With head held high, she stormed out the door and across the busy office, aware of eyes following her all the way. At the glass door she turned and looked back, her gaze sweeping scathingly over the room, stopping abruptly on the tall, gray-suited figure watching her from a doorway. He was too far away for her to read his expression, but she had no doubt but that he was congratulating himself on getting rid of her so efficiently.

But he hadn't seen the last of her, Juli thought grimly. Not by a long shot.

Chapter Two

The tires squealed as Juli's little car shot out of the parking lot. Her thoughts were wildly incoherent. He had accused her of trying to *cheat* the company! Of all the incredible, insufferable nerve — how dare he! And all the time *he* was the swindler, stealing David's invention and cheating Aunt Kate out of what was rightfully hers. Grabbing Juli's shoulder as if she were some sort of thief — warning her! Angrily, she realized she hadn't even had a chance to tell him what she thought of Taylor Electronics' truck drivers who hogged the highways.

She was back at the bridge over the dry riverbed before she calmed down enough to realize she was headed in the wrong direction to find David's trailer. She retraced her tracks, still fuming, and finally found Reynaldo Road. It was a pleasant, older street lined with orange trees, some still holding colorful balls of fruit. She drove along slowly, watching for David's address number. Farther out the sidewalks disappeared and the houses were shabbier and farther apart. The paved street dwindled to gravel and then, to Juli's dismay, to dirt tracks that followed a ridge of yellowish boulders into the desert.

A few mailboxes gave evidence of habitation, but the houses were hidden in the dips and rises. The desert was neither as level nor as barren as it had appeared from a distance. Juli recognized the tall, stately saguaro cactus from pictures she had seen, as well as the paddle-shaped prickly pear cactus. But more numerous than either of these was a particularly vicious-looking cactus with angled branches entirely covered with golden thorns.

Juli had almost decided she had somehow gotten on the wrong road and was ready to turn back when she spied one last lonely mailbox leaning crookedly by the side of the road. On it was the name "Flynn" in faded red letters, the last "n" drooping, as if the painter had miscalculated and failed to allow room for it. David, Juli remembered with an affectionate sigh, had never cared much about appearances.

That fact was even more apparent after Juli cautiously guided her car over the rocky driveway and finally spied the trailer parked in a flat, bare area out of sight of the road. No effort had been made to make it look pleasant or homey. It just sat there, a pink and aluminum colored metal box with an air cooler, like some sort of ugly growth, on the roof. A nearby saguaro offered only a few fingers of shade.

Juli tried to swallow her dismay. She fished the key out of her purse. It had been sent to Aunt Kate along with a few other personal things of David's after the accident.

She wrinkled her nose at the heavy smell of stale air when she opened the door, and her eyes widened at the sight of the disarrayed interior. Clothes flung over a chair, piled carelessly in a corner, draped from doorknobs. Books everywhere. A shelf with several of David's whimsical contraptions that had fascinated Juli as a child, dust-covered and motionless now. Sink full of dirty dishes. Counter incongruously littered with chunks of rock.

Juli, for a few awful moments, thought the trailer had been ransacked or vandalized, but on closer inspection she realized it had not. This was simply the way David had lived, and housekeeping obviously was not one of his priorities.

She picked her way across the gritty

floor and opened the windows. The outside air, if not cool, was at least fresh. She went on through the trailer, opening bathroom and bedroom windows. David had evidently taken up rock collecting, because there were several cardboard boxes of rocks stacked in the bedroom.

She felt almost guilty as she surveyed the unmade bed, as if she were peering into an area of David's life where she had no right to be. He wouldn't have liked the intrusion.

But it couldn't be helped, she sighed to herself. The bedroom had an exterior door and she opened that, too, trying to get some circulation going in the stuffy air. In back of the trailer she saw a dilapidated shed, a pole with some sort of electrical box fastened to it, and a makeshift clothesline.

It all had such a forlorn look, and Juli was suddenly angry again. Did Thorne Taylor pay so poorly that this was the best David could afford? And now he was trying to cheat David even further. It wasn't fair!

She hurried out to the car and lugged her suitcases inside, again surprised by the heat at this time of year. She was perspiring lightly by the time she changed into denim shorts and halter top with bare mid-riff. She had felt a little foolish packing such clothes with snow on the ground back in Ohio, but she was certainly glad she had them now.

After changing her clothes, she found clean linens in the bathroom and made up the bed. She was relieved to find the electricity had not been shut off. There was no telephone, but there was water in the faucets, and the refrigerator, though desperately in need of cleaning and defrosting, was also working. With a few days' work she should be able to get the trailer into condition presentable enough that it could be offered for sale, she decided. She poked around in closets and finally found a vacuum cleaner stuffed behind a pile of shoes.

In spite of the vacuum cleaner's location and the general appearance of the trailer, both of which hinted that the machine was seldom used, the paper dust bag was full and she couldn't find another. She felt damp and dirty by the time she gave up looking. She tried the air cooler but quickly flipped the switch off when the cooler made a few definitely unhealthy sounding groans and shudders. Finally, she went outside, brushed sand off the trailer steps, and sat down. She felt wilted and dispirited.

From here she could see the trailer windows were filthy and would have to be washed. The screen door needed repairing. David's talents had been in the scientific field, not carpentry, and the steps were definitely wobbly, too.

The enormity of the task ahead of her suddenly seemed almost overwhelming. Even more overwhelming was the question of what to do about Thorne Taylor's total rejection of her claim that Aunt Kate had something coming to her. Should she see a lawyer? She had recklessly warned him that Aunt Kate was ready to sue the company, but the more she thought about it, the more she suspected any reputable lawyer would reject the claim as too flimsy. Thorne Taylor seemed to have everything on his side: David's signed agreement with the company, Juli's own lack of information about what David had invented, Thorne Taylor's obvious wealth and power, plus the force of his personality and physique. Juli suddenly felt shaky just at the thought of going up against him in a legal battle.

Or any kind of battle, she thought uneasily, massaging her sore shoulder lightly.

The faint bluish shadows of bruise marks from the powerful grip of his fingers were already beginning to show on her fair skin. But deeper than the bruises was the memory of those gray-green eyes burning warningly into hers. She shivered suddenly in spite of the heat.

He had deliberately kept her waiting, she decided, thinking back. It put him in control of the situation; *he* was the one who kept people waiting, and he certainly hadn't apologized when he did arrive. What was his noon meeting that had run overtime? Juli suddenly suspected that it might well have been a private, not business, matter. In spite of the hostility and cold contempt he had shown toward her, Thorne Taylor was far too attractive to devote all his time and attention to the electronics business. What sort of woman would attract the interest of a man like Thorne Taylor?

With an unexpected warmth, she suddenly remembered the way his eyes had boldly appraised and classified her as attractive. But she also remembered how he had carelessly dismissed that observation. Merely being attractive wasn't enough to warrant Thorne Taylor's interest, of course. He could have his pick of any number of attractive girls, and no doubt amused himself with more than a few of them, she thought disdainfully. No, it would take more than merely being attractive to warrant any *real* interest on Thorne Taylor's part.

She jerked her mind away from that distracting line of thought and back to the problem at hand. If it weren't that Aunt Kate desperately needed financial assistance, she would be tempted just to forget the whole matter. Even if he were totally in the wrong, Thorne Taylor was almost too clever, too powerful to fight.

And yet, considering that David had signed that paper, wasn't it true that Taylor Electronics was both legally and morally entitled to anything David invented or discovered while working for the company? The thought that *she* might actually be in the wrong had not occurred to her before, and it was a disquieting idea.

She rejected it quickly. David had sounded too positive that Taylor couldn't cheat him "this time." Which must mean, of course, that Thorne Taylor had somehow cheated him previously.

She realized her thoughts were right back where they had started. Sighing, she went back inside and started cleaning out the smelly refrigerator, wincing once when the door accidentally struck her sore shoulder. She realized she should have picked up supplies at the grocery store, but she didn't feel like driving back for them now. The smell of the moldy, spoiled food in the refrigerator, plus the unpleasant after-taste of her meeting with Thorne Taylor, hadn't left her with much appetite, anyway.

The boxy metal trailer seemed to retain heat even after the air began to cool a little outside. She contemplated tackling the stack of dirty dishes but decided to wait until the trailer cooled off. Glancing outside, she suddenly realized a few clouds had drifted in and there was going to be a spectacular sunset.

Her Polaroid camera was still in the car. She got it and snapped a shot of the trailer with the sun behind it. The result wasn't what she wanted, and she looked around for some better vantage point to get the full effect of the colors.

The view from the boulder-strewn ridge would be perfect, she decided. If she hurried, she could make it there in time to get several good shots as the sunset colors changed.

She hurried out to the road, but within only a short distance it ended in a dusty turn-around. She struck off toward the boulders on what she hoped was a trail. She hadn't gone far before she realized she was poorly dressed for a desert walk. Her bare legs seemed almost to invite attack from the golden-thorned cactus, and she had to watch every step she took in the flimsy sandals to avoid stepping on the older, dead clumps of cactus needles littering the ground. She stopped to rest beside a low, bushy tree and found that it, too, was sticky.

Not exactly a hospitable place, she thought wryly, rubbing a stinging scratch on her bare leg. A man named *Thorne* ought to feel right at home. And yet, in spite of the inhospitality of rock and cactus, the desert had a certain harsh, alien beauty, as if it had been painted with a different but no less appreciative brush than the green farmland back home. Here the colors were neutral ochres and umbers, burnt siennas, weathered yellows, and dusky browns. The golden-thorned cactus, lovely but vicious as a lurking predator, dominated the landscape, but there were also thick stubs of barrel cactus and waving whips of yet another thorny plant. Over all towered the magnificent saguaros, arms bent or twisted as if signaling some indecipherable but timeless message. She had read some saguaros were upward of a hundred fifty to two hundred years old, and it gave her a feeling of awe to think they had been standing right here when Indians and whites battled over the land.

She knew she probably should turn back. The ridge of boulders was farther away than it had looked from the trailer, the desert distances being deceiving. But she had come this far and she was determined to go on. By now the sunset promised to be even more glorious than she had expected, a burning glow of red and gold like some ancient sacrificial fire smoldering on the horizon.

She struggled on, clambering over boulders that at some time in the past had thundered down from the ridge. Above her the yellowish rocks turned to a glowing gold in the rays of the sinking sun. She wouldn't have much more time before the colors faded.

Finally she reached a huge, rough-surfaced boulder balanced almost precariously on top of the ridge. Again, the desert had deceived her and the ridge was higher than it had appeared from a distance. The trailer below looked small and lonely. Without waiting to catch her breath, she hastily untangled the camera strap from around her neck and aimed directly at the sinking sun. Without waiting for the colors to develop on the Polaroid print, she snapped two more shots.

By that time the first print was beginning to develop. She held it between thumb and forefinger, disappointed. The sunset colors were appearing, but she had angled the camera, giving the landscape a peculiar tilted look. The second print was blurred, as if she had moved at the moment the shutter snapped. The third shot was the best, but she was still disappointed with it. Somehow, it had simply failed to capture the glorious beauty her eyes could see.

As she held the prints, waiting for them to develop fully, she suddenly had the odd, uncomfortable feeling she was being watched. She glanced around uneasily, realizing how alone and vulnerable she was in this isolated spot.

She saw the camera first. It was set up on a tripod, fully equipped and obviously expensive. It was partially concealed by a clump of desert shrubbery, but if she hadn't been so engrossed in snapping her own pictures, she would surely have seen it earlier. But who . . . ?

And then she saw him.

He was leaning against another boulder, naked to the waist, arms crossed against powerful chest. Sculptured shoulder muscles tapered down to hard, flat waist. Lean hips, molded thighs . . . In the golden glow of the setting sun, he was a bronze statue, a pagan desert god of virility. He moved and the muscles rippled under the sheen of bronzed skin. Juli swallowed convulsively and lifted her eyes to the lean face. There was something almost satanic about the faint, sardonic smile, the bronze glint of the hair. The sinking sun played shadows like firelight across his skin, shadowing his eyes as he moved toward her. A desert devil come to life against a flaming sky . . .

"I expected we would meet again, but I didn't realize it would be so soon."

Juli gasped and blinked as reality collided with that mesmerizing image of gleaming bronze sculpture. "Mr. — Mr. Taylor! I didn't recognize you —"

He raised a dark eyebrow. "Without my clothes on?"

She felt her face flame. "No! I didn't mean that —" He was quite decently covered, of course. She could see now that the dark material that molded his muscular thighs was not some satanic garment, but merely an old pair of jeans.

"Sorry," he said without sounding particularly apologetic. "I was swimming. When I realized the sunset was going to be worth photographing, I just threw on a pair of pants and grabbed my camera." The faint smile was sardonic again. "I'd have dressed, of course, if I'd realized I was going to have such attractive company."

"I . . . I just wanted to take some photographs, too — something to take home to David's mother," Juli said shakily. He was standing beside her now and she found his nearness disturbing. There was a primitive masculinity about his bared chest, a virility to which she had to fight back an unfamiliar, almost shocking response.

"May I see your photographs?" He held out his hand and reluctantly she handed the Polaroid prints to him, careful to avoid touching his lean, capable fingers.

"They aren't very good," she said apologetically.

He inspected the photographs and handed them back without comment. She knew he didn't think they were good, either, and his superior attitude annoyed her.

"I'm sure I could do much better, of course, if I could afford the fancy, expensive equipment you have," she snapped.

He waved a tanned hand toward the tripod. "Help yourself."

He had neatly trapped her, of course. She bit her lower lip. She hadn't the faintest idea how to operate a camera that required more than the most simple of adjustments.

He picked up her camera from where she had set it on a flat rock, inspected it briefly, and then eyed the western sky. Only the rim of the sinking sun remained, a dying red glow. He peered through the viewfinder, looked around, moved a few feet away, and kneeled down. A minute later he stepped back and handed the stiff, slick Polaroid print to her.

She held it, silently watching the colors develop. His hand had been rock-steady, no trace of a blur. By kneeling, he had silhouetted a saguaro against the dying glow of the sun and somehow captured both the sunset beauty and the harsh, alien landscape of the desert.

"It's very nice," she murmured. Defensively, she added, "Perhaps I should have waited until the light was different."

"A moment ago you seemed to think your equipment was at fault." His voice was taunting and he had trapped her again, she realized angrily. She reached over and snatched her camera back. "It isn't the price of the camera that is the most important factor in taking effective photographs, Miss Townsend," he said pointedly. "It is the skill and judgment of the person behind the camera."

So he was a better photographer than she was, Juli acknowledged. Did that give him the right to go around acting so superior? And what did he mean he was out here "swimming"? There couldn't be enough water out in this dry desert for a minnow to swim in. And yet his crisp hair was definitely still damp. She was almost going to ask, but decided against it. She swung the camera strap around her neck and turned around, looking for the way she had climbed the ridge.

His voice stopped her. "Miss Townsend, I'd like to talk to you a moment."

His voice was neither loud nor demanding, but there was something compelling about it. Reluctantly, Juli turned and looked at him again. The sun was gone now and his body no longer gleamed like that of bronze god. But he was no less magnificent as a mortal man, a man vitally alive, humanly virile.

"About what?" she finally managed to ask warily.

"After our . . . uh . . . discussion earlier today, I talked with Dr. Johnson and went over the research department records. I thought perhaps David had accomplished something of which I was unaware. However, I'm afraid I could find nothing to substantiate your claim that he had recently made some sort of 'scientific breakthrough' or invented anything of particular value to the company."

"I doubt that you were looking for anything to substantiate *my* claim," Juli retorted scornfully. "I imagine you're doing everything you can to protect your own interests — no matter how unfair that might be to others."

Even in the gathering dusk she could see the tightening of his chiseled lips, but his voice was controlled when he spoke. "At the time of his death, in fact, David was involved primarily with the testing of some of our new products, not with actual research," he stated.

"David was brilliant and creative. He could do more than test products."

"Brilliant, true," Thorne Taylor agreed. Bluntly, he added, "But unreliable."

"Unreliable!" Juli gasped furiously. "So,

you're not only going to cheat David's mother out of what she deserves, but you're going to indulge in character assassination, as well — against a man who can hardly defend himself!"

"Miss Townsend, I assure you —"

Juli refused to listen anymore. She turned and started down the slope, suddenly aware of how rapidly darkness was falling. With the setting of the sun, the desert air was surprisingly chill, too. She heard him call again, but she plunged ahead, dodging the needle-sharp thorns that clutched at her from all directions. But in her anger she had forgotten that she must also watch where she stepped, and a moment later a searing pain stabbed through her left foot.

Involuntarily she cried out and instinctively grabbed at her foot. The hot-needle pain bit into her hand and a dozen horrifying thoughts flashed through her mind — spider, scorpion, tarantula! Wildly, almost hysterically, she shook her hand, trying to free it from that stinging grip.

Suddenly a strong hand caught her flailing wrist. "Stop it. *Stop it!*" he commanded harshly.

"Something bit me!"

"No. It's only a piece of cholla. Calm down."

Doubtfully, Juli peered at the sticky clump clinging tenaciously to her hand. It was true. It was just a bit of the thorny cactus caught on her hand. "Cholla?" she repeated uncertainly.

"The cactus for which the town is named. Not without good reason, I'm sure you'll agree," he added dryly, indicating the sticky sea of golden-hued thorns around them. "Painful, but not deadly."

Juli felt a little foolish making such a fuss over nothing more than a cactus, but that didn't lessen the searing pain in both her hand and foot. She blinked back tears and reached for the sticky clump with her other hand.

"Don't do that." His hand tightened on her wrist. "Cholla has a spine barbed like a fishhook. It sticks to anything it touches."

Juli had already experienced that unhappy fact. When she jerked the sticky clump away from her foot, it had only clung to her hand. Now both felt as if red-hot needles had been driven into her flesh.

He looked around. "Over here," he said.

She hobbled after him as he led her by the wrist. He guided her hand to a flat rock.

"This is going to hurt," he warned.

She gritted her teeth and nodded. He

used a stick to press the cholla against the rock and then pulled her hand away. He was right. It felt like a dozen fishhooks ripping through her flesh.

"Sorry," he said gruffly. "That's the only way to do it."

She was glad the thickening darkness concealed the tears spilling out of her eyes. "Thank you," she said stiffly. "I'll be more careful in the future." She held the torn, burning hand with her free one to still its trembling. Somewhere she had lost the Polaroid pictures she had taken, but she didn't care. All she wanted now was to get back to the trailer. She took a step in that direction, only to feel the searing pain shoot up her leg again. One of the cholla spines must still be embedded in her foot.

"Where do you think you're going?" he demanded. "You can't make it through there alone."

In dismay Juli realized that the faint trail she had followed up to the ridge had been swallowed up in deepening shadows. Lights twinkled from the town off to the south, but the area below the ridge was completely dark. With a sense of panic, she realized she wasn't even sure where the trailer was located.

But if Thorne Taylor thought she was

going to beg him for help, he was mistaken, she thought resolutely. If it took her all night to find her way through this maze of cactus, she'd still do it. She took another step, gritting her teeth against the pain.

"You're being foolish," Thorne Taylor's voice chided. "Just because you want to get away from me —"

"I don't want to get away from you!" Juli snapped. She broke off angrily. That hadn't come out right. Lamely, she added, "I mean, I do, but —"

She realized she was standing on one foot, keeping her weight off the other one. His sharp eyes saw it, too.

"Okay, that's enough," he said decisively. "I'm not going to have you adding some sort of personal-injury suit to the one you already have planned."

"Mr. Taylor, I assure you I have no intention of suing you because I stepped on a piece of cactus!" Juli said indignantly.

"Just to make sure —" He took a long stride toward her and before she had any idea what he intended, he reached down and swept her up in his arms. She was too astonished to protest for a moment. She felt the strength of his arms cradling her, felt the even more intimate warmth of his naked chest against her bare midriff. In the growing darkness her body was a pale contrast to his deeply tanned skin, his hand a dark print on her bare leg. He started through an opening in the boulders with her, and she finally came to her senses enough to voice an enraged objection.

"Mr. Taylor, put me down! *Now!*" she demanded.

He didn't reply, simply tightened his arms and pressed her even closer to him in order to squeeze through the narrow passageway between the jumbled rocks. Her cheek was against his shoulder, her breasts crushed against his chest. Her anger at this cavalier treatment was suddenly joined by a feeling of panic. Where was he taking her? What did he have in mind? She knew little about what kind of man he was, except that David had distrusted him. And that he seemed totally indifferent, or deaf, to her protests.

She twisted and struggled in his arms, kicking wildly until his powerful grip clamped her legs so tightly together she couldn't move. "Mr. Taylor, you have no right — I insist — put me down!" she gasped breathlessly. Taking a different tack, she added, "Your camera —"

"I'll come back for it later. No one is going to be up here to steal it." His voice sounded calm and under perfect control, in distinct contrast to her breathless gaspings. The only effect of her struggles on him was a thick strand of dark hair falling across his forehead. It brought back that faintly satanic look.

She peered around trying to memorize the route he was taking in case she had a chance to flee. They were going downhill now, through more boulders on the far side of the ridge. She marked a peculiarly twisted saguaro outlined against the sky. He seemed to know the area well, moving forward without hesitation. Her only view was back over his shoulder at the boulders and cactus silhouetted behind them.

Where could he be taking her? she wondered frantically. A parked car seemed the most likely answer. She did not find the thought reassuring.

Suddenly the trail, if it was a trail they were following, twisted, and she had a view in the opposite direction. To her surprise the lights beyond this side of the ridge were far more numerous than on the other side, and the regular pattern indicated a subdivision or housing development of some sort. And to her greater astonishment, directly below them were the faint outlines of a large, sprawling house and the glow of outdoor lights on a swimming pool that gleamed like a turquoise jewel. This, she knew instantly, was no subdivision tract house.

Thorne Taylor set her down on a cement patio built into a natural recess among the boulders. A drooping tree that looked faintly golden in the glow of the pool lights hung over one edge of the patio.

"Where are we?" Juli gasped. It was a little like walking into a desert mirage that had somehow turned into reality.

"My home." He shrugged, the arrogant eyes looking down at her. "You were, as a matter of fact, trespassing on my property."

Juli suddenly realized that even though he had set her down, she was still clutching his arm and leaning against him. She jerked away self-consciously, only to feel the pain of the embedded cholla thorns shoot through her foot again. In dismay, she realized that somewhere in her struggles she had also lost the sandal on that foot. She brushed an unruly tendril of hair out of her eyes.

"I'm sorry about the trespassing," she said with all the aloof dignity she could muster in her disheveled condition. "Now, if you would just tell me how to get back to the trailer — ?"

"I'll drive you," he said briefly, "after we take a look at that foot. And a little antiseptic on your hand might be a good idea, too."

Juli thought about protesting, but there didn't seem much point in it. She could hardly make her way back through the cactuses barefoot, and by now the foot throbbed sickeningly. He opened a door into a dimly lit rear hallway. Juli hobbled past him without meeting his eyes. He helped her down the hallway with a firm hand on her elbow. Juli didn't want to accept his help, but it was either that or hop along in a most undignified manner.

They passed through a kitchen with a hooded, island stove and rich pecan cabinets. Copper-bottomed pans gleamed on one wall. They went down another hall lushly carpeted. The hallway opened on what appeared to be a comfortably casual family room looking out on the lighted pool. The pool, like the patio in back, was built to blend in with the natural setting of the gigantic boulders, and a palm tree leaned gracefully over the jeweled water. Inside the room there was a large, rock fireplace, handsome, wood-beamed ceilings, and sofas and chairs in pleasant, earthy colors.

"Wait here. I'll get a first-aid kit," Thorne Taylor instructed.

Juli looked down at her feet and legs in embarrassment. They looked like those of a child caught playing in the dirt. The scratch on her thigh was beaded with dried blood. She had forgotten all about it. "Is there someplace I could wash up first?"

He helped her down the hall to the most luxurious bathroom she had ever seen outside of a beautiful-homes magazine. The floor was of Italian tile, and there was a double, cultured-marble sink, the entire wall above it being mirrored. The lighting was concealed, soft, and flattering. Lush ferns almost covered a frosted window, and live vines grew around the sunken tub. The room had a sensual, almost jungle, feeling.

"My mother dotes on bathrooms," he said with a shrug.

Juli looked around uneasily. She didn't like the idea of being alone with Thorne Taylor, but in her present condition the idea of encountering his mother was even less appealing. "Does she live here?" Juli inquired.

"When she isn't jetting off to some other part of the world. She's in Acapulco with some friends right now."

Juli felt relieved.

"There's soap and towels," Thorne Taylor indicated. His appraising glance traveled over her. "Go ahead and take a shower if you'd like."

Juli stiffened. "I don't think —"

"The door has a lock," he pointed out sardonically. "And I'm not in the habit of getting kicks by playing peeping Tom in the shower."

Juli felt her face flame as he backed out of the door and pulled it shut behind him. In the huge mirror she could see that her face looked as pink as it felt. She could also see that his appraisal was justified. She needed a shower. It wasn't only her feet and legs that were dust-covered. But still, taking a shower in the home of a man she barely knew . . .

Recklessly, she slipped out of the shorts and halter, though not before making sure the door was securely locked. She stepped under the stream of hot water, a little embarrassed at the muddy puddle that gathered around her feet in the elegant tub. She hurriedly rinsed off and rubbed herself dry with a luxuriantly thirsty towel. She disliked slipping back into the shorts and halter, though perhaps as much for their skimpiness as their smudged condition.

The warm water felt soothing, though

the foot still throbbed. She could see the embedded stickers, but she had no luck trying to dig them out. Reluctantly, she realized she was going to have to accept Thorne Taylor's help. For a moment she wondered why he was helping her at all when he thought she was trying to pull some shady trick on his company. Then she remembered his wry comment about the possibility of her also filing a personal-injury claim against him because she had been injured on his property. He was only protecting himself. She found the thought oddly disappointing.

He was waiting outside the door with a first-aid kit. He had, she noted with a certain unexplainable relief, added a shirt that covered his bronzed chest. He warned again that this was going to be painful, and it was, but with deft hands and tweezers he finally managed to pull the barbed spines out. He applied antiseptic to the foot, dabbed more on her hand, and for good measure swabbed off the scratch on her thigh. In spite of the sting of the antiseptic, Juli was more sharply aware of the disturbing feel of his hands on her skin.

"Thank you," she finally managed to say when he finished up with Band-Aids. With an attempt at lightness, she added, "I promise not to sue you."

He snapped the first-aid kit shut. His eyes, so intent on her injuries a moment earlier, were now partly speculative, partly amused.

"I mean, not about this, anyway," she added lamely, remembering the other matter.

"I didn't think I was going to get off that easily," he said dryly. But with a hardening voice, he added, "But I meant what I said. A legal battle will not be pleasant."

Juli suddenly felt both foolish and guilty discussing a legal battle while sitting here in the comfort of his home with the feel of his competent hands still warm on her skin. "I'd like to go home now, if it wouldn't be too much bother," she said in a small voice.

For a moment Juli thought he was going to pick her up and carry her again, and her heart unexpectedly pounded erratically at the thought, but he merely aided her with his hand on her elbow. Outside he helped her into a low-slung silver Porsche.

It turned out to be a rather long drive, since they had to circle all the way around the long ridge. The road had several dips in it where it crossed old washes, though there was no water to be seen now. Finally, he pulled into the rough driveway that led to the trailer and braked beside her little car. In the glare of the headlights, the trailer looked even more lonely and forlorn than it had earlier. Not a light was to be seen on the desert floor around them, and on the horizon the jumbled boulders had strange, menacing shapes. Juli hesitated, oddly reluctant to leave the car.

"I see you know where David lived," she remarked finally. She had not given him directions to reach the trailer.

"As a matter of fact, I didn't know until I was going through his file today and saw the address. Then I realized his must be the trailer I could see from my ridge."

"Did you see me walking up the slope to the ridge?" Juli asked suddenly.

In the glow of lights from the instrument panel he seemed to hesitate, then nodded.

"You could have called out and told me I was trespassing," she pointed out.

"I suppose so." He shrugged. "Frankly, I didn't think, dressed as you are, that you'd manage to get all the way to the ridge."

His eyes moved over her again and Juli suddenly felt vulnerably exposed and acutely conscious of the way the halter top revealed the curve of her breasts.

"You're a very determined young woman, aren't you?" he added unexpectedly, his voice contemplative.

She knew he was not referring merely to her climb up the cactus-covered slope. "I . . . I like to see justice done. If my Aunt Kate has something coming to her, I intend to see that she gets it. But I am not out to 'con' your company out of something!" she added heatedly.

"You don't know yet how long you'll be staying?"

"No. Actually, I've thought a little of moving out here. The insurance company I work for has a regional office in Phoenix. I could get a transfer."

"Oh?"

He sounded politely disinterested, and Juli wondered angrily why she had blurted that out. It had been only a passing thought, anyway, not something she was seriously considering. And certainly not something about which *he*, president of Taylor Electronics, would care about, one way or the other.

"Of course, that was before David's accident," she added hastily. "I have Aunt Kate to consider now." She pushed the door handle down to let herself out. "Thanks for . . . for everything."

He was fingering the keys in the ignition,

a faint scowl on his face. He glanced over at her. "Juli, I've been thinking. It's possible that David was working on something of his own here at the trailer. He was a loner and kept to himself. It might be worth your while to search though his things. I assure you, if you discover something David was doing on his own, Taylor Electronics will make no claim on it."

Juli looked at him, lips parted in surprise. It was not a thought which had occurred to her, but, knowing David as she did, the idea seemed a distinct possibility. Not that she'd know what she was looking for among his things, of course, but it was considerate of Thorne Taylor to make the suggestion. She wondered if he realized he had called her *Juli*, not the usual, mockingly formal *Miss Townsend*.

"Thank you," she said again. "I appreciate the suggestion."

He waited until she was inside and had the lights on before turning the car around in the yard. She watched as the red taillights receded down the bumpy road. Had she misjudged him? Was he really concerned and trying to be helpful?

Or was he, she wondered doubtfully, merely trying to divert her attention away from his company's underhanded doings?

Chapter Three

Later, after a supper of canned soup and stale crackers, Juli lay in bed aching with weariness and yet unable to sleep. Was she being unduly suspicious of Thorne Taylor, unfairly accusing him? Had David had an exaggerated idea of the value of something he had done for the company? Or had David, as Thorne suggested, been working on some project of his own here at the trailer? And if that were true, how had Thorne and Taylor Electronics cheated David in the past?

Her feelings toward Thorne were confused, the anger and hostility she had felt earlier confronted by her disturbing awareness of his powerful masculinity, his smoldering virility. A shiver of sensual awareness went through her as she remembered the heat of his lean, bronzed body pressing against her bare skin when he had carried her. Later he had called her "Juli," speaking her name as if it came naturally. The shiver changed to a warm softness that spread through her body, a seeping tide of drugging, honeyed warmth.

She dashed the tantalizingly pleasant feeling with the cold water of reality. Nothing had really changed. He had made no concessions, admitted nothing. Thorne Taylor was still her adversary, and she must not let her purpose here be distracted by the treacherous response of her senses to that devastating combination of the savage and sophisticated in him.

It was a restless night. She awakened once to a howling and yipping that some basic, primitive instinct within her recognized as coyotes wailing, even though she had never heard them before. Another time something scratched against the trailer. Heart pounding, she peered out, only partly relieved when she saw the whip-like tentacles of a desert plant brushing against the metal of the trailer. The moon had risen and it was an unreal landscape outside, all silver and shadows, the dark silhouettes of saguaro as menacing as an army of alien beings advancing through a sea of gleaming cholla. Not a light was visible from her window, only the vastness of the desert. She shivered, suddenly cold in her filmy nightgown.

In the morning, of course, everything

looked different. One of the first things she came across as she hung her clothes in the closet was a book on desert vegetation. She took it outside, wandering around in the pleasant warmth of the morning sunshine to compare the living specimens with photographs in the book. The tentacled plant which had scratched against the trailer was an ocotillo, not a true cactus in spite of its heavily thorned branches. She identified the tiny hedgehog cactus, growing in clumps, one with an astonishingly large magenta-colored bloom. There was the creosote bush, one of the hardiest and most common plants of the desert, with its tiny yellow blossoms. The book said the waxy-leaved jojoba bore a fruit that early settlers had ground up and used as a coffee substitute when the real thing was unavailable. The golden-hued tree overhanging Thorne's patio had evidently been a native palo verde, Arizona's state tree. She was surprised as she wandered around at the number of birds singing and swooping among the seemingly inhospitable desert plants.

Reluctantly, she gave up her pleasant browse through the desert and drove into town to buy supplies and get on with her task here. The markets had a marvelous array of lush fruits and vegetables, and she went overboard buying tiny, sweet tangerines, pink-fleshed grapefuit, shiny green peppers, and red-ripe tomatoes. She picked up cleaning supplies and found a store which sold bags for the vacuum cleaner. She visited the electric company to bring the bill up to date and make sure the electricity would not be turned off. When she inquired about a water bill, she was told the trailer must be supplied by a well on the property because city water service did not yet extend out that far.

That was evidently true, she decided later as she peered into the shed out behind the trailer. She didn't see a pump, though she ruefully realized she might not know one if she saw it. There was an upright water tank, and since water seemed to be reaching the trailer faucets satisfactorily, she decided not to worry about it. More boxes of rocks half-filled the shed. Juli could not imagine why David had bothered gathering such a dull, unremarkable collection.

Later, however, she had a sudden inspiration about what to do with all the rocks. She arranged them in a neat row to outline a walkway from the trailer steps to the parking area, then used the remainder to mark off a small yard in front of the trailer. She was pleased with the results. The area immediately looked neater and more cared for, and the small barrier seemed somehow to hold the vastness of the desert at bay.

She worked diligently inside the trailer for several days, cleaning, scrubbing, sorting, throwing away. She kept an eye out for anything which might indicate David had been doing private research here at the trailer, but she found nothing. She half-hoped Thorne would contact her or come around, but she heard nothing from him. Every once in a while she found her gaze straying to that ridge of jumbled yellow boulders, wondering what he was doing on the other side, but there was never any sign of him, and she determinedly tried to busy her thoughts elsewhere. The wounds on both her hand and foot were healing nicely and gave her no problems. There was a surprisingly heavy downpour of rain one night, but otherwise the weather was balmy and she quickly acquired a honey tan.

By the weekend it seemed obvious she was not going to hear anything from Thorne Taylor, and she was undecided about what to do next. There were still some things of David's to sort through. He was always writing notes to himself, and it appeared that he never threw anything away. She even ran across the birthday card she had sent him last year. She thought, however, that the trailer was now presentable enough to list with a real estate agent.

On Saturday morning she decided the first thing to do was telephone Aunt Kate, back in Ohio. She hated to let Taylor Electronics win without a battle, but so far it appeared she hadn't much ammunition with which to do battle. Her thoughts were further complicated by her decidedly ambivalent feelings toward Thorne Taylor himself. On a rational, mental plane, her feelings hadn't changed. She still felt suspicious of him, annoyed with his arrogant air of superiority and angry that he seemed untouched by Aunt Kate's plight. But underneath, on some more elemental level, her senses refused to recognize him as anything but a virile, capable, dangerously exciting man, a reaction that both puzzled and dismayed her.

She placed the call from a telephone booth outside a downtown drugstore. It went through quickly, without complications. She barely had time to tell Aunt Kate that she was fine when the older woman interrupted excitedly.

71

"Juli, you're a marvel! I don't know what you said to Taylor Electronics, but it certainly got results!"

In astonishment Juli listened while Aunt Kate went on to say that just that morning she had received a letter from Taylor Electronics offering her a generous sum of money.

"For what reason?" Juli cut in.

"Oh, I'm not sure. 'A goodwill gesture in consideration of the death of your son while employed by the company,' or something like that. They said they weren't admitting any liability for his death or anything, and that seems reasonable enough. It was David's own car and he was driving at the time of the accident, so it certainly wasn't the company's fault. That Mr. Taylor sounds like a very nice man. Have you met him?"

"Yes, I talked with him," Juli acknowledged noncommittally, her mind elsewhere as she considered the sum of money the company had offered Aunt Kate. As a "goodwill gesture" it was indeed generous, and yet . . . Then her mind fastened on that one word. "You said he *offered* you this money. What does he want in return?"

"Why, nothing, really." Aunt Kate sounded slightly offended, as if Juli had

72

criticized David himself. "There was just some legal paper saying I'd accept the money and wouldn't make any further claims against the company, or something like that. You know how confusing legal papers are. I just signed and sent it right back."

"Already?" Juli gasped. "Without getting legal advice?"

"I thought the sooner I returned it, the quicker I'd get the money. I'm behind on so many bills," she said, sounding defensive. Anxiously, she added, "You do think I did the right thing, don't you?"

There was little point in upsetting Aunt Kate by scolding her for what was already done, Juli sighed to herself. The legal form was already signed and on its way. Juli murmured something noncommittal and they chatted a bit longer about the weather and selling the trailer, improvements in Aunt Kate's control of her left side, and the possibility she might be able to eventually work part-time.

But when Juli hung up the phone she was seething with anger. No wonder Thorne Taylor had urged her to spend her time — *waste* her time! — searching the trailer for something that wasn't there. That gave him time to buy off Aunt Kate

73

and get her signature on some sort of release form so there was no possible chance of further legal action being taken against the company. No matter what he'd said to Juli, Thorne Taylor obviously knew David had invented something of great value to the company. And Juli had no doubt but that the sum offered to Aunt Kate, generous as it might seem to her, was a mere pittance compared to thc true value of David's invention. A mere fraction of what Thorne was afraid Aunt Kate might win if the case went to court!

And there was nothing she could do about it now, Juli thought in furious frustration as she slid behind the wheel of her car. Nothing! Thorne had won, slick and smooth, without so much as a line of worry to mar those handsome features.

Oh, but there was one thing she could do, she thought grimly as she headed out Reynaldo Road toward the trailer. Abruptly, she spun the steering wheel and turned to circle around the long ridge of yellowed boulders. She could tell Thorne Taylor exactly what she thought of him and his sneaky, underhanded tricks!

She tore along the uneven road, hurtling heedlessly into the dips and over the rises, her mind concentrating on what she in tended to say. No need for tact or diplomacy now, only the truth of what a despicable, detestable, greedy, underhanded —

Her thoughts broke off and she slowed her headlong rush as the road narrowed to a driveway that passed beneath an elegant wrought-iron archway. She had not seen this in the darkness that previous evening. Nor had she seen how the driveway circled around to enclose a natural park-like grove of cottonwoods, with trails laid out among clumps of mesquite and palo verde. Off to one side was a wooden-fenced arena with a couple of horses lazing in the sunshine and a neat stable behind them. A walkway curved gracefully to the recessed entryway in the house. The landscaping was an attractive blend of native desert plants and carefully tended evergreens. A splash of red bougainvillaea brightened a wall that evidently concealed the swimming pool.

Juli hesitated, suddenly feeling at a disadvantage barging in like this. She hadn't dressed to go into town and make the phone call; she had merely slipped on a clean pair of jeans and a scoop-necked peasant blouse. Thorne might not be home. He might be entertaining guests.

No, she chided herself angrily. She was

rationalizing, letting his home and status overwhelm her. Defiantly, she parked her dusty car directly in front of the house and slammed the door behind her. She didn't care how elegant his home was, or how smooth and sophisticated he might be; she intended to give him a piece of her mind. And if he wasn't home, she just might barge right into Taylor Electronics' smoothly purring office and say what she had to say where everyone could hear!

She stormed up to the door and jammed her forefinger on the doorbell before she could change her mind. A chaotic jumble of angry words tumbled on her lips. As the door swung open she struggled to compose herself, determined not to come across in some way that Thorne Taylor could derisively dismiss as feminine hysterics.

"Yes?"

Juli stared, the angry words caught in her throat. The young woman who stood in the doorway was a few years older than Juli and obviously not a maid or hired help. She had sleek, dark hair pulled back from an oval face, expressive dark eyes, flawless skin tanned to a shade that was more golden than brown, and sculptured lips. She wore a white terry-cloth beach jacket that only partially concealed a slim but full-breasted figure in a striking, one-piece black bathing suit that plunged below her nipped waist-line. The tiniest hint of a frown touched the woman's smooth forehead, and Juli realized in embarrassment that she was standing there gawking foolishly.

"I — May I see Mr. Taylor, please?" Juli asked awkwardly.

"I'm sorry, but he isn't here right now," the young woman said coolly.

"Will he be returning soon?" In a rush, Juli added, "Or perhaps I could catch him at his office later." In the face of this woman's cool, assured beauty, Juli suddenly felt sweaty and disheveled.

"Both the plant and office are closed today. If you're looking for employment, you'll have to see the personnel office on Monday." The woman's voice was polite, but there was a hint of condescension in it. Unhappily, Juli realized she probably looked as if she needed a job.

"Well, I . . . I'll just catch Mr. Taylor some other time, then," Juli said. Lamely, she added, "I'm not looking for work."

"May I tell him who called?" the woman inquired. She lifted an elegantly arched eyebrow questioningly, her dark eyes both curious and appraising. "Was he expecting you?"

"No, no, he wasn't expecting me." Juli started backing toward the walkway. She didn't intend to ask the question that was on the tip of her tongue, but the words just burst out. "Who . . . who are you?"

The sculptured lips curved into a self-possessed smile and the dark eyes widened. "Why, I'm Mrs. Taylor, of course."

Juli just turned and fled, crawling behind the wheel of her little car and turning the key with a damp, tremulous hand. Thorne was married! Why hadn't he told her? Her face burned as she suddenly remembered those strange, unfamiliar feelings he had aroused in her as she lay in bed at night, tossing and turning as she remembered the devilish glint of his eyes and that smoldering virility she had never sensed in any man before. How dare he let her think —

A car was coming under the arched entrance as she careened down the driveway. A silver Porsche. They met just inside the gates. She felt a moment of pure panic, a desire simply to stomp the gas pedal to the floor and flee, to deny even to herself that she had ever had those wild thoughts about a man who was not only despicable in his business dealings, but who was also *married*.

Then a cold determination to do what

she had come for swept over her. She was not going to let him get away unscathed with cheating Aunt Kate. She was aware that something new was added to her anger now, but she refused to acknowledge even to herself that the unexpected news that Thorne was married had anything to do with her intensified desire to lash out at him.

She braked and eyed him coolly. The windows of both cars were open. He was so close she could have reached out and touched him — or slapped him, she thought grimly, almost aching to feel the sting of her palm against that lean, hard cheekbone. He smiled, a brilliant flash against sun-darkened features.

"I didn't know you were coming or I'd have made it a point to be here. I don't like to miss a visit from a beautiful young lady."

The warm words and flashing smile caught Juli off guard and she had to steel herself not to respond to them. What was he trying to do now? Charm her into submission the way he had evidently charmed Aunt Kate in his letter?

"Is something wrong?" he asked, his manner turning wary when she didn't respond to the smile.

"I understand you've written to my aunt," Juli said, keeping her tone and expression under tight control.

He nodded, regarding her thoughtfully. "The company tries to be fair. We decided, in this case, that a payment to a surviving family member was justified."

"Justified!" Juli repeated scornfully. "You buy off Aunt Kate with a fraction of what she should have received, and then —"

"Now just one minute, Miss Townsend!"

"Yes, I know — we can't do anything now that you have her signature on your clever little legal document, but that can't keep me from telling you what I think of you personally, Mr. Taylor! You're cheap and cruel and greedy and underhanded —" Descriptive words failed her and she broke off, breath coming in harsh jerks. "And I hope you choke on every cent you stole from her! You know David invented something valuable to the company, or you would never have paid her and tricked her into signing the release form." She launched into another torrent of angry words describing his seedy character and morals.

She could see the expression on his face change from wariness to surprise and then to harsh, set anger as the chiseled lips tightened grimly and a muscle jerked along the lean jawline. She was aware that the tight control under which he was holding himself might explode at any moment, but she was beyond caring.

When she ran out of breath, he said grimly, "Miss Townsend, I think there are a few things we should discuss. Now, if you'll calm down, so we can —"

"I have no intention of calming down or discussing anything with you!" Juli said wildly. "And it was *Juli,* not Miss Townsend a few nights ago when you sent me off on a wild-goose chase digging around in David's things so you'd have time to pull your underhanded deal on Aunt Kate. And you didn't even let me know you —" Juli broke off suddenly, biting back the words about learning he was married, refusing to let him know that mattered one way or the other to her.

"Miss Townsend, we are going to discuss this," he said grimly. "Now, if you'll just pull your car over there so we aren't in the middle of the driveway —"

"No," Juli snapped. "I'm leaving."

His gray-green eyes narrowed. "I don't think so," he said flatly. Without taking his eyes from hers, he reached for something on the dashboard, and in astonished dismay Juli saw the iron gates swing shut directly in front of her car.

"I should have realized the electronics expert would have some toy like that to play with," she jibed, her voice scornful in spite of the panicky pounding of her heart.

He ignored the taunt, motioning to a parking place beneath a spreading cottonwood. "Over there."

Juli hesitated a moment, but she didn't seem to have much choice. The gates were shut tight and obviously wouldn't open again until Thorne chose to open them. She could only make herself look foolish with further protests. She backed up the car, then swung under the cottonwood. Thorne was already standing beside the Porsche when she slid out of her car. He was wearing dark slacks and a knit shirt that molded to his muscled chest. She resolutely put down an inward, primitive surge of attraction she felt toward him.

Without speaking, he took her elbow and guided her to a planked table and benches a short distance down a graveled trail. The harsh grasp hurt, but she refused to give him the satisfaction of complaining. She sat stiffly on the bench, as far away from him as possible.

"What did you want to discuss?" she

asked distantly. She didn't look at him, keeping her eyes focused on the horses lazing in the corral, though what she was really seeing was a seductively rounded figure in a black bathing suit, sculptured lips saying calmly, "Why, I'm Mrs. Taylor, of course."

"I don't understand your attitude toward my communication with your aunt," Thorne began, his voice warily reasonable. "The company had no legal obligation to pay her anything."

"And so you're sending the money out of the goodness of your heart," Juli said sarcastically. "Pardon me, but I can't quite swallow that. I think the fact that you offered her payment, in return for her signature on some legal form, proves exactly what I've believed all along — that David did invent something of particular value to the company. And that the payment you're making is a mere pittance compared to the value of —"

"We've been through this before. You have an extremely exaggerated idea of David's contributions to the company," Thorne cut in. His voice hovered on the brittle edge of exasperation, the end of patience. "I take it you haven't found anything in the trailer to suggest he was doing something on his own that the company didn't know about?"

"You didn't really think I would, did you?" Juli retorted.

His chiseled lips compressed into a thin line as he studied her. His long legs were stretched out in front of him, arms folded across his chest. He was wearing boots, burnished from use and age, but still retaining their look of expensive elegance. "I'm trying to be reasonable about this," he finally said tightly. "But you're making it very difficult."

"In other words, I'm not as cooperative as most of the women you encounter," she suggested derisively.

He eyed her as if suspecting there was a double meaning in her words, that she was not referring entirely to business dealings. "And just what do you mean by that?" he challenged boldly, dismaying her with his directness.

Juli bit her lower lip, wishing she had never made the remark. She did not care to get into a discussion of his marital status, particularly when she suddenly suspected that in spite of his wife's attractiveness, he probably did exactly as he pleased where other women were concerned. He had certainly shown no hesitation about carrying her into his home that evening, an act that would have given most married men at least momentary pause for thought. And his eyes had told her more than once that he found her attractive. Even now, as he scowled at her with ill-concealed impatience and anger, she could feel a super-charged current of pure sexuality sparking between them. And this practically under his wife's classically beautiful nose!

Unexpectedly, he slid across the smooth surface of the varnished bench and tilted her chin up, forcing her eyes to meet his. "I asked you a question," he said, his voice softly dangerous. "I have the feeling I'm being accused of something. I want to know exactly what it is."

He was so close she could feel the warm brush of his breath on her lips, see the pulse beating in his throat, breathe the faint hint of a masculine after-shave lotion. She clenched her fists until the nails dug into her hands, hating herself for the way her heart thundered in response. He was married!

And yet . . .

She felt a soft weakness that started somewhere deep inside flood through her in a warm tide, a tide that swept away the blaring warning signals in her mind. His lips were no more than inches away from hers, and her eyes drifted shut as some relentless, inevitable force pulled them together. . . .

And then, over his shoulder, through half-closed eyes, Juli saw her. The bathing suit had been exchanged for hip-molding jeans and Western shirt, but there was no mistaking the sleek, dark hair and slim but full-breasted figure. She was walking across the corral, horse halter in hand, and the chestnut gelding whinnied a familiar greeting.

Juli jerked back, eyes suddenly wide open, her breath caught as if she had just stepped back from a precipitous dropoff. She had almost — how could she! Shame flooded through her.

"What's wrong?" Thorne demanded angrily.

Wrong! Juli repeated incredulously to herself. He, a married man, was trying to kiss her, almost in full view of his wife, and he was asking what was *wrong?*

"Maybe you ought to ask Mrs. Taylor!" Juli flung over her shoulder as she strode toward the car. "And I don't mean your mother!"

He caught up with her in a few long

strides. "Juli, what in the world —"

He reached for her at the same moment she twisted to grab the car-door handle. His hand caught the neckline of her peasant blouse just as she jerked the door open. The noise of cloth ripping sounded as loud as a gunshot.

They stared at each other and then he slowly released the torn material and withdrew his hand. For a moment Juli was too shocked and horrified to move. Then she clutched frantically at her torn blouse, struggling to conceal the lacy wisp of her exposed bra.

"How — how dare you!" she gasped.

The astonishment in his eyes was only momentary, quickly replaced by a stubborn glint. "I didn't know you were going to —"

She slammed the door shut and started the car, cutting off anything he might say. She struggled with the steering wheel, awkwardly trying to keep herself decently covered at the same time. Her glance darted between the rearview mirror and Thorne leaning against the silver Porsche with what seemed insolent nonchalance, considering that he had just practically ripped off her blouse. Her palms and back were almost instantly damp with nervous perspiration, but he watched her with an infuriating calm.

She finally gave up trying to wrestle the car backward into the main part of the driveway and jolted forward to drive around the full circle that led past the house. From there she could see Mrs. Taylor saddling the horse, looking not only beautiful, but efficiently competent. Juli scrunched down in the seat, only hoping her disheveled condition could not be seen. She had never felt so embarrassed, so totally humiliated. She speeded up as she headed toward the arched entryway, wanting only to get away from here as fast as possible. She glanced toward the cotton-woods, warily watching for Thorne's tall figure but catching only the silvery gleam of the Porsche.

And then, as her eyes darted back to the driveway, she realized the reason for his air of nonchalant superiority. She had for-gotten all about those closed gates! They loomed ahead of her like prison bars, spike-tipped and unyielding. She braked, all concern with keeping herself decently covered forgotten as she used both hands to try to control the skidding car. She could never stop in time —

Chapter Four

The car vibrated with the force of the skid, the wheel shuddering in Juli's clenched hands. And then, only seconds before impact, the spiked iron gates swung outward and the car skidded on through. It came to a dead stop on the sandy shoulder of the road. Juli rested her head weakly against the wheel, mind frozen, hands limp and nerveless now. Her mouth felt dry, her throat too tight to swallow at the realization that only split-seconds had separated her from disaster. She drew in a deep, shuddering breath, her stomach suddenly giddy with nausea. If Thorne hadn't managed to open the gates just in time . . .

But following that thankful thought came a rush of angry realization. There had been plenty of time for Thorne to open the gates! It was obvious she intended exiting when she circled the driveway. And yet he had chosen to leave the gates closed, stubbornly barricading her way. Only when impact seemed inevitable had he finally relented and activated the gate controls from his car.

And that probably not so much for her sake as to prevent his expensive gates from being damaged, she thought cynically as she lifted her head from the steering wheel and dried damp palms on her jeans. She caught a glimpse of movement in the rear-view mirror and hurriedly fumbled with the ignition key. She had no intention of staying around for some derisive comment from Thorne on her driving ability.

The engine growled ominously for a moment, but then caught, and she pulled back onto the road. She drove slowly, aware of one side of her lacy bra exposed by the torn blouse, but too shaky to take a hand off the wheel to hold the ragged edges of material together.

A little farther on, realizing she had to pass through the streets of the housing development, she pulled off to the side of the road and found an old jacket on the back seat with which to cover herself. Her hands were trembling now, fury and shock and humiliation all mixed up together. From the very first she had sensed that savage part of Thorne hidden beneath the sophisticated exterior of the respected business leader, and today the veneer had fallen away to expose his character, as he had exposed her body. And all within shouting distance of his wife. She looked again at the ruined blouse, the naked skin of her shoulder, and the upper curve of her breast. How could he — how dare he!

She drove on home to the trailer, thoughts in turmoil. There she showered in the rickety metal shower stall and tried to calm her shattered nerves. She had two primary thoughts. One was that Aunt Kate was lucky to get anything from Taylor Electronics, considering today's exhibition of this violent aspect of Thorne's character. The other was that all she wanted now was to get the trailer and property sold and get away from Cholla as quickly as possible.

With that thought in mind, she made a strong cup of coffee to strengthen her shaky nerves and forced down a tuna sandwich. For the first time since arriving in Cholla, she slipped into a dress, a full-skirted apricot-colored sundress that complemented her brown hair and glowing tan. Somehow she felt the odd need to both look and feel feminine, as if that could somehow erase the morning's shocking confrontation with its undertones of raw sexuality. Juli could not imagine any of the men she had dated back home ever doing such a thing, at least not by anything other than pure accident, and then with embarrassed stammers of apology. But then, she thought grimly, she had never gotten involved with a man like Thorne Taylor before.

She selected a real estate agent at random, pulling over to the curb when she spied the sign between a drugstore and a florist's shop. She entered without hope of selling the property for more than a minimal sum, and the salesman seemed unimpressed when she showed him her Polaroid snapshot of the trailer. She explained briefly about David's death and the circumstances of the sale. He nodded and um-hmmed without much enthusiasm, murmuring that they didn't get much call for small trailers. But when she told him the address, his interest perked up.

While he went across the room to locate property maps of the area, Juli became aware of curious glances from a customer talking to a salesman at another desk. The man was of medium height, wearing a slate-blue suit that looked almost too suave among Cholla's mostly casual dressers. He was a few years older than Juli. He wasn't pale, but he hadn't the outdoorsy tan that was so customary here. He wasn't handsome, either, but he had an interestingly angular face and alert blue eyes. The salesman pushed a photograph across the desk to him. He returned it with a disinterested shake of his head.

Juli's salesman returned then. His manner had changed completely. He pointed out the property on the map. It was larger than Juli had realized. Hesitantly, she asked his advice about a suitable selling price and his answer astonished her.

"That doesn't seem possible! We never expected anything close to that."

He went on to explain that the area was expected to be annexed to the city soon, and a property the size of this could then be subdivided into home sites.

"Way out there?" Juli asked, still astonished. "It's just dry desert."

The salesman smiled. "Well, as the sign says, Taylor Electronics is bringing progress and prosperity, and Cholla is growing right along with the company." He turned the map around. "In addition, you're fortunate that the property is out of a flash-flood area. Builders have to watch that. Some of these dips and washes may look as if they've been dry for a hundred years, but once in a while we get a real 'gully-washer' of a rain. I'd say your cousin made a pretty shrewd buy, getting that piece of land before values went up."

Juli suspected David's purchase of the land was not so much a shrewd investment as a facet of his solitary character and a desire to be as far away from neighbors as possible, but she didn't say anything.

"You could probably get more for the place if you want to hold it until the annexation goes through," the salesman added, "but if you're in a hurry to sell —"

Juli nodded firmly. "I'm in a hurry." She hesitated a moment, eyeing the blue lines on the map indicating property borders. "Does the property join the Taylor land?"

The salesman nodded and grinned. "Which doesn't hurt its value, either," he said. "Too bad it's on the wrong side of the ridge, or the Taylors themselves might be interested."

They settled on the asking price and the salesman jotted down a few more details. Juli started toward the door, pleased. The money from the sale, plus what Taylor Electronics was paying, would set Aunt Kate up quite nicely, especially now that she might be able to work part-time. Juli was just reaching for the door when an arm reached around and opened it for her.

"Please, allow me," the man who had been at the next desk said. He smiled. "It's so nice to see a girl who looks all frilly and feminine. I get a little tired of athletic Western girls in pants who always look as if they're ready to rope a steer or brand a cow."

Juli returned the smile. What he said was an exaggeration, of course, but it did give her spirits a nice lift. She murmured a thanks, letting it cover both the compliment and his courteous gesture. She started toward her car, not interested in furthering the acquaintance, but his next words stopped her short.

"I didn't mean to eavesdrop, but I couldn't help overhearing. I'm Brian Eames. I was hired to take David Flynn's place at Taylor Electronics."

The shocked look on her face brought another apology to his lips. Stunned, Juli just looked at him. Her first reaction was an illogical surge of anger, like hearing of a first wife replaced by a second before the grave is hardly covered. No one could take David's place! But she quickly realized the unfairness of that, and with it came another thought. Brian Eames worked in the very job David had held. If anyone was in a position to know what David had done, it was this very man. If she could obtain inside information, perhaps a way could be found to circumvent that paper Aunt Kate had signed. If she could prove that Thorne and Taylor Electronics deliberately deceived or defrauded Aunt Kate —

Juli gave Brian Eames her warmest smile and he stopped apologizing, seemingly a little dazzled. Guiltily, Juli realized she wasn't being quite honest, that there was an ulterior motive behind her sudden change in attitude, but she determinedly shoved the guilty feeling aside.

"Somehow I didn't think you were a Cholla native," she said lightly. "You're from back East?"

He nodded. "Shows that much, does it? Well, I can't say I'm sorry," he said cheerfully. "A tan is fine, but I prefer broiling a thick steak to overcooking my own skin — though I must say you've reached a very appetizing state of doneness," he added, eyeing her honey tan appreciatively.

Juli just laughed. "Are you buying a home here?"

"Thinking about it. Even if I don't stay here too long, a house should be a good investment, the way prices keep going up. I don't have a wife or family," he added.

Juli eyed him reflectively. His comment

96

that he might not be staying long interested her. Did he already have a grudge
against Taylor Electronics? She wondered
what to say next, now definitely wanting to
prolong the conversation. Brian Eames
made that easy.

"Could I interest you in joining me for a
nice cool margarita in the lounge around
the corner?"

Juli had never in her life accepted the
offer of a drink from a man she had just
met under such casual circumstances, nor
did she have any idea what a margarita
was. But she recklessly nodded yes. If there
was a chance to find out something which
might be useful in her battle against Taylor
Electronics, she was not going to let the
opportunity slip by.

She left her car parked where it was.
Brian stopped to throw a real estate pam-
phlet into his car. It was not as luxurious
and expensive a model as Thorne's
Porsche, but it was low-slung and sporty.
He touched her elbow lightly as they
rounded the busy corner. Juli hesitated
once, thinking she saw a familiar silvery
flash among the cars passing by on the
street, but a passing truck blocked her view
before she could be certain.

The lounge was cool and dim, soft music

coming from some unseen source. The tables were almost unoccupied at this hour. He guided her to a secluded table in a corner and ordered two margaritas. They chatted conversationally about the weather, local property values, exchanging impressions of Arizona in general. Juli was anxious to work the conversation around to the subject of David and his job, but she didn't want to be too obvious about it. The drinks arrived and Brian took a quick, appreciative gulp of his.

"Ah," he said. "Lovely. Margaritas and air conditioning are all that make Cholla bearable. Of course, that was before I met *you*," he added, inspecting her with unconcealed interest.

Juli smiled and eyed the frothy, delicately green-tinted drink doubtfully. "What is it?"

"Mostly tequila and lime juice. Try it. It's much better-tasting than it sounds."

Juli sipped tentatively, surprised to find the sweetly tangy taste quite pleasant. She touched the rough salt crystals rimming the curved glass. "Salt?"

He nodded. "The rim of the glass is rubbed with lime juice and then dipped in salt," he explained. "Of course, the *real* way to drink tequila is to sprinkle the salt on the back of your hand, take a sip of tequila, and then have a lick of salt. Somewhere in there you're supposed to suck a lemon, too. However, the more civilized among us, including myself, prefer the salt-dipped rim. And lime juice."

Juli wrinkled her pert nose and laughed. "That does sound a bit more civilized."

"And sanitary," he added. He leaned forward. "I hate to say this, but I hope your cousin's place doesn't sell too soon so you'll stay around for a while."

It gave her the smallest crack of an opening. "I think David must have liked it here. Or perhaps it was the job he liked, more than the town."

"It's a good job, all right," Brian admitted. "Taylor Electronics pays well. But then they'd have to, to get anyone to stay in this godforsaken place."

It was on the tip of Juli's tongue to say that she found Cholla quite pleasant and, given a little time, thought she could learn to love the harsh, dry beauty of the desert. But she held her tongue, not wanting to get sidetracked on that line of discussion. "You said you were doing David's job?" she prompted.

"In a manner of speaking. His death created a vacancy in the department, and I was hired to fill it. However, David was involved in product-testing at the time of his death, and I've since moved over into actual research."

"Oh." Juli felt vaguely disappointed. That was the same story Thorne had told her. She sipped the cool, refreshing drink, wondering if she dared come out with what was really on her mind. Would Brian Eames be interested in helping her?

"I understood that the company expected great things of David when they hired him, but from what I hear he had other things besides his job on his mind."

"What do you mean?" Juli questioned cautiously.

Brian's brow wrinkled slightly and he shrugged. "Actually, I'm not sure. David was such a loner that no one seemed to know much about him. Maybe he got involved with a woman. Or drinking. Who knows? But he had something on his mind. However, I can't say I'd condemn a man for resorting to some vice to make life bearable here." He paused suddenly, blue eyes intent. "I hope I'm not upsetting you. I don't mean to."

"Of course not," Juli assured him. As a matter of fact, she reflected, what Brian was saying could be a confirmation that David had been on to something big and important, something that preoccupied both his time and interests. Could it have been something secret, something other workers in the department didn't even know about?

"If you'd like a tour through the plant or the research department while you're here, I could arrange it," Brian offered unexpectedly.

Juli shook her head, restraining a shiver. "I don't think so. I've already met Mr. Taylor."

"Ah, yes," he said dryly. "Our suntanned leader. Cholla's most eligible bachelor. One glance from him and fourteen secretaries swoon at their desks."

One word leaped out at Juli. "Bachelor? But I thought he was married!"

Brian shook his head. "Not unless he acquired a wife since yesterday. And I'm sure that didn't happen, or there would have been a groan of disappointment from the secretarial pool that could have been heard all over Cholla."

Juli ignored his facetious exaggeration. "But I just met his wife," she protested. "I had to go to . . . to Mr. Taylor's house for something, and she was there. And she definitely said she was *Mrs.* Taylor."

Brian asked Juli to describe the woman.

Juli did so in as straightforward a manner as possible, giving a general description of age and coloring without remarking on the woman's seductively sexy appearance.

Finally, Brian nodded. "Oh, that was Mrs. Taylor, all right. Mrs. Nicole Taylor. She's the widow of Thorne Taylor's younger brother, Jason."

"Widow!" Juli gasped. "But she said —" Juli broke off, surprised and puzzled. She was sure the other woman had deliberately led her to believe she was Thorne's wife.

"You've seen the Taylor place?" Brian asked, eyeing her with frank curiosity.

"A little business matter concerning David," Juli explained hurriedly. Her mind was spinning. What Brian was saying didn't change what Thorne had done, of course, but it threw a subtly different light on the situation. Thorne might be arrogant and savage, but he hadn't been sneaking around behind a wife's back. "Was Thorne's brother involved in the company, too?"

"Oh, sure. Half-owner. He did a lot of traveling for the company, I understand. He died several months before David's accident."

Brian's second drink arrived and he gulped it as appreciatively as the first. With it came crisp tortilla chips and a creamy guacamole dip. The rich blend of avocado and spices was a perfect contrast to the icy drinks, but Juli's thoughts were elsewhere.

"How did he die?" she asked curiously.

"Hiking accident. It happened up in the Superstition Mountains. He had a hobby of hunting for lost gold mines, and there's supposed to be a famous one up there somewhere. He slipped on a rock or something and fell over a cliff. Some other hikers saw it happen, but he was dead when they got to him."

Juli shuddered. "How awful."

Brian nodded. "Just one more reason you won't find *me* stumbling around out there. But the widow seems to be bearing up nicely," he added dryly. "With Thorne Taylor's strong arm for support, of course."

Juli glanced up sharply. "Is there something between them?"

Brian shrugged. "You hear all kinds of rumors."

"Such as?"

"The talk is that they're just waiting for a decent interval of time to elapse after Jason's death before she becomes Mrs. Thorne Taylor."

"I see." Juli put her drink down. Her

stomach felt suddenly queasy. "I take it they're not concerned with how it looks with her already living there under the same roof with him."

"She doesn't live there," Brian corrected, "at least not yet. She has a home up in Scottsdale, near Phoenix. Another estate, from what I hear."

"You mean she and her husband lived up there even though the company is permanently located here? I wonder why," Juli mused.

Brian nodded. "I think a lot of people wondered the same thing. Of course, there are any number of reasonable explanations."

"Such as?" Juli prodded again. She had the feeling Brian Eames was rather enjoying feeding her this information bit by bit.

"As I said, Jason traveled quite a bit, so perhaps there simply was no need for him to maintain a home here. And then some people say Nicole Taylor refused to live in Cholla, that she preferred the more active social life Phoenix and Scottsdale have to offer. If that was the reason, I can sympathize with her feelings."

Juli waited, twisting the salt-rimmed glass nervously. She suspected there was more. There was.

"And some people say that Jason simply refused to let Nicole live down here."

"Why?"

"It seems Thorne and Nicole had a pretty hot thing going before she married Jason. In fact, everyone expected Thorne and Nicole to get married. But all of a sudden she up and married Jason instead. Rumor has it that Jason wanted to keep as much distance as possible between Thorne and Nicole."

"But surely Thorne wouldn't go after his own brother's wife," Juli protested.

"No? Perhaps Jason knew his brother better than you do." Brian's laugh was cynical. "But from what I hear, Jason wasn't any too successful at keeping Thorne away from his wife. A few miles aren't about to stop a guy like Thorne Taylor."

Juli's heart flip-flopped. "Wh-what do you mean?" But she didn't have to hear Brian's reply to know the answer to that question, of course. Thorne had been playing around with Nicole Taylor even while her husband was alive. "Thorne Taylor sounds like quite the lady-killer," she murmured, trying to keep her voice casual, "what with keeping all those swooning secretaries busy and chasing after his brother's wife, too."

"Actually, much to their annoyance, I

think he has kind of a hands-off policy to-ward company secretaries," Brian con-ceded. "He does his playing around where it won't disrupt company business. And where marriage is concerned, he has his eye on bigger game, of course."

"Of course," Juli echoed hollowly. She toyed with the melting ice in her drink. "I presume Mrs. Taylor inherited her hus-band's half of the business."

Brian nodded. "Right. And you can bet Thorne isn't going to let that get out of the family."

Juli remembered her own earlier thoughts that mere physical attractiveness wouldn't be enough to interest Thorne Taylor. She had been right. Nicole wasn't merely attractive; she was stunning, plus being poised and elegant. And she owned half the company. It was an irresistible combination. "You seem rather well in-formed about everything, considering you haven't been with the company very long," Juli commented with a sideways glance at Brian.

He laughed. "There isn't too much to do here *but* talk about each other," he pointed out. With a suggestive quirk of an eyebrow, he added, "And I always like to know where the skeletons are buried. You never know when a little information may come in useful. Right now, for instance," he added.

Juli felt a momentary twinge of distaste. She had never been one to indulge in the idle gossip that made the rounds of the insurance office where she worked, and she did not find gossiping particularly attractive or admirable. But then she had to admit her own guilt. She had certainly prodded Brian for every bit of information he had given her. She flushed when he commented on that, also.

"You seem rather interested in the local goings-on yourself," he suggested speculatively.

"It's just because of . . . of something to do with David," Juli said evasively. And that was true, she assured herself. She had no personal interest in Thorne Taylor's relationship with his brother's widow, past or present. And yet there was one more question.

"I wonder if Nicole is here now to announce the engagement."

"Could be. But the company's annual picnic and barbecue is next weekend. She could be here to help with the arrangements for that. I gather it's the big social event of the year." He paused reflectively.

"That might be when they'd choose to announce the happy news, of course. Everyone troops out to the Taylor estate and they barbecue a herd of cattle or something."

Juli couldn't help laughing at his obvious exaggeration. She took a sip of her drink. "You don't sound very enthusiastic," she commented.

He wrinkled his nose. "I have the feeling it's the kind of thing where you're expected to spear a chunk of meat and eat it at a dead run on horseback, or something barbaric like that."

"I don't think it could be *that* barbaric." Juli laughed.

"You don't think so? Then you don't know our Thorne Taylor. Don't let his sophisticated appearance fool you," Brian warned. "He's not one of your tame, domesticated types, as Nicole Taylor may soon find out."

Juli shivered, her smile suddenly mechanical as she remembered the way Thorne had savagely ripped and ruined her blouse. Yes, she had no doubt but that he could be barbaric, indeed.

She drained her glass, intending to excuse herself, but her eyes widened as over the rim she saw a powerful figure standing at the door. There was something almost menacingly predatory in the way his eyes swept over the room. Brian's back was to the door and he didn't see. He talked on, but the words rolled meaninglessly over Juli as Thorne's eyes unerringly found hers even in the dimness of the room. For one heartstopping moment Juli thought he was going to stride over to the table, but with a motion that shouted pure disdain, he spun on his heel and disappeared.

What was he doing here? Was he alone? He had departed instantly upon seeing her, almost as if —

"Are you all right?"

"What?" Juli's eyes wavered and finally refocused on her companion.

"You looked so strange for a moment — almost as if you were ill."

"Oh, no, I'm fine," she assured him. "It just seems a little cool in here after being so warm outside," she improvised. "You were saying — ?"

"I was just suggesting perhaps we could have dinner together. The restaurant here isn't any match for New York's finest, but it's not bad. At least they don't drown everything in grease and chili sauce."

Juli's heart was unexplainably pounding, and her hand trembled as she replaced the glass on the table. She had held it to her mouth so long while her eyes locked with Thorne's that the taste from the salt-rimmed glass clung to her lips. She licked them lightly, remembering with an odd tremor how close Thorne's lips had come to her own not more than a few hours ago.

"Let's make a deal," Brian said suddenly, eyeing her closely. "No more talk about the Taylors or Taylor Electronics. I get the feeling that for some reason you find the whole subject upsetting."

"Only because I . . . I don't feel they treated David fairly," Juli said faintly. "I really couldn't care less about their personal relationships. And dinner sounds lovely," she added determinedly.

They ate at the restaurant adjoining the lounge. Brian ordered chicken Kiev, which Juli had to admit looked marvelously succulent and delicious. But she, much to Brian's disgust, she suspected, chose one of the Mexican specialty dinners and enjoyed spicy stuffed peppers called *chiles rellenos, frijoles refritos,* crunchy jicama salad, and warm, soft tortillas. For desert there were *sopaipillas,* fluffy golden pillows stuffed with sweetened fruit jam. At the end Juli surreptitiously licked the last delectable bit of sticky jam from her fingertips.

By that time she was almost relaxed, the tense feeling that Thorne Taylor might somehow barge in at any moment finally disappearing. She could almost feel sorry for Nicole Taylor, planning to marry such a headstrong man. They finished the meal with strong, savory coffee, and Brian entertained her with anecdotes about local people and events, humorous, though a bit biting at times. She gathered he regarded his position with Taylor Electronics as primarily a stepping stone to bigger things with a company more desirably located.

After dinner Brian walked her back to her car. Juli was surprised to find it was almost dark outside. She shivered lightly in her bare-shouldered sundress.

"I don't suppose you'd be interested in a movie, would you?" Brian asked hopefully.

Juli shook her head. "Thanks, anyway, but I —"

"I know. I've already monopolized more of your time than I had any right to on such short acquaintance. Perhaps if I could call you — ?"

"I'm sorry, but there's no phone at the trailer. I guess David didn't feel he needed one."

"That fits in with what I've heard about David, all right. He wasn't very sociable."

The comment gave Juli an opening and quickly, without explaining too much in detail her reasons for wanting to know, Juli asked Brian if he could find out a little more about David's work at Taylor Electronics. She said that any information he could gather could be very important to her.

Brian looked curious, but seemed agreeable enough. "Now I have a favor to ask of you," he returned. "How about coming to the company picnic and barbecue with me next Sunday? I wasn't planning to attend, but together we might get some laughs out of it."

Juli hesitated, torn by conflicting feelings that had nothing to do with Brian. Attending the barbecue would mean seeing Thorne again. One part of her shrank from that prospect. He was a ruthless, determined man who let nothing stand in the way of what he wanted. He might not be married at the moment; he might even be interested in Juli in some temporary, very physical basis. But marrying Nicole Taylor was his real plan, a plan with which Nicole seemed in perfect agreement. Risking any involvement with him could only mean heartbreak for Juli.

And yet, in spite of what had happened

today, another part of her traitorously tingled with excitement at the prospect of simply being near him again.

"I promise to be a good sport. I won't complain even if we have to rope our meal on the hoof." Brian grinned and Juli guiltily realized he thought her delay in making up her mind had something to do with seeing him again.

Now rationalization took over. She had to see Brian again in order to find out if he had learned anything helpful to her. She might, at a gathering of company employees, even find out something useful on her own.

She smiled at him, quelling a shivery feeling inside, a feeling that was a strange blend of apprehension and anticipation. "I'd love to go with you."

Chapter Five

Juli paced the trailer restlessly before Brian arrived on Sunday to take her to the barbecue. Thorne's flowers werc in a quart jar on the dinette table, no vase available among David's haphazard assortment of utensils. The other part of Thorne's gift was tucked into her purse for return to him. The more Juli thought about it, the more infuriated she became over what he had done. It was insulting and degrading. If it were not that she was determined to return what Thorne had sent her, she would have called off going with Brian today.

As it was, she had already nervously changed clothes twice. The backless coral dress she had bought for the occasion somehow looked far more daring and revealing now than it had in the store. She had put it on, uneasily changed to slacks, and then defiantly slipped into the dress again. What would Nicole Taylor be wearing? Something stunning, no doubt. Would she and Thorne take the occasion of this big company event to announce their engagement? Maybe she wouldn't have to stay, Juli thought suddenly. If she could catch Thorne alone for a moment and say what she had to say, she and Brian could just slip away. She doubted that Brian would be disappointed. He still looked on this whole affair as some sort of barbaric Western rite akin to throwing sacrifices to idols.

Brian whistled approval of the new dress when he arrived. On the drive over to the Taylor estate, he filled Juli in on what he had been able to learn about David's work at the company. It was not particularly encouraging, although it appeared that in the early days of David's employment he had done quite well and even picked up a small bonus for an innovative design change. But he had gone downhill from there. He often left work early on Friday afternoons and sometimes didn't return to work until Tuesday. He was, in fact, close to being fired at the time of his death.

"I'm sorry," Brian apologized. "I don't know exactly what you wanted to hear, but I doubt that this was it."

He was right, of course, and Juli felt more bewildered than ever. If everything Brian said were true, why had Thorne bothered to offer Aunt Kate anything? And how, under the circumstances, could David have written that glowingly optimistic letter to his mother? Juli also wondered, as she had before, what he did with his money. Brian had implied that the job paid well, and David certainly hadn't been *overly* generous with his mother. Was it possible he did have some secret vice?

As they passed under the arched entryway, Juli resolutely put those thoughts and questions out of her mind. She had another little matter of importance to take care of here today.

The park-like area within the large circular driveway was already overflowing with people. A table had been set up for food and drinks, and a whole series of long tables and benches were scattered around to provide eating space. A portable playground had been brought in for the children, and the gate to the swimming pool was wide open. A loudspeaker blared rollicking country music from a small band playing near the barbecue pit. Brian braked to avoid a very small boy on a long-legged horse trotting across the driveway. A herd of noisy, bathing-suited kids stormed toward the pool. Brian said something, but his words were drowned out by

116

the whinny of a horse practically in Juli's ear. The aroma of meat cooking and chili simmering mingled with the smell of sweaty horses and dust. An American flag waved in the breeze; beneath it was a green Taylor Electronics banner.

Juli felt an unexpected tingle of excitement at the hustle and bustle, the noise and smells and music and laughter. Everyone was obviously having a good time. She craned her neck to watch a group of kids on horseback inside the corral playing what seemed to be a form of musical chairs, astonished at the way the riders flung themselves off their horses and scrambled for seats when the music stopped. It seemed miraculous to her that there were no broken bones or other casualties.

Brian, grumbling, squeezed his gleaming, freshly washed sports car into a parking space between a dusty horse trailer and a battered pickup. They walked back toward the tables. Everyone seemed to have a soft drink or beer can in hand, but evidently the food wasn't being served yet. An arm-wrestling contest was going on at one table, and another group of people was playing horseshoes. Juli had the uncomfortable feeling of being overdressed. The garb of the day seemed to be Levi's and green T-shirts with the Taylor Electronics emblem emblazoned on the back. Except for Brian, of course, and even his casual leisure suit looked too formal.

Then Juli spied Thorne. He was supervising the removal of the meat from the barbecue pit. Juli had to admit Brian had been right about one thing. It was more meat than she had ever seen at one time. At least a half, maybe even a whole, side of beef had been cooked in the pit. Thorne was wearing the same jeans and T-shirt as everyone else, but even so, there was something about his powerful physique and authoritative air that made him stand out from the crowd. And where, Juli wondered as she glanced around, was the shapely Nicole?

"Well, well, our illustrious leader displays another talent," Brian remarked derisively as he watched Thorne.

Juli felt a small flash of annoyance. Brian didn't need to be quite so disparaging about *everything*. It was rather generous of Thorne to open his property and provide all this for his employees. But then she scoffed at herself for even momentarily defending him. Thorne probably cold-bloodedly put a dollar value on buying employee goodwill this way. He had certainly seemed to think he could buy her!

"I suppose he'll whip out his camera to record all this for posterity," Brian added. "That's another of his talents."

"Oh?" Juli said, curious in spite of herself.

"He's rather well known for his desert photography. He's had quite a few photographs published in *Arizona Highways* and won some awards."

So that explained why he was up on the ridge taking photographs that first night she had encountered him, Juli realized. She also suspected as she glanced at Brian's slightly scowling face that he was probably envious of Thorne and his talents and accomplishments. She knew the feeling, she thought ruefully, thinking of Nicole being not only gorgeous but a company owner — and competent with horses, besides.

At that moment the object of Juli's thoughts walked up and put her arm through Thorne's with a possessive gesture that indicated she owned not only the company, but Thorne, as well. She was wearing the uniform of the day, but hers were designer jeans with saucy little red hearts appliquéd to the rear, and she filled

119

out her T-shirt with voluptuous fullness. Her hair was loose and tousled, and she did look stunning, though in a rather different way from what Juli had expected. Again Juli felt uncomfortably overdressed.

"Well, what do you think? Is she wearing a bra or isn't she?" Brian commented appraisingly.

For a moment Juli was shocked by Brian's remark, but then she realized it was just part of his generally derisive air, an air she was beginning to realize he put on because he felt uncomfortable and out of place.

"I'm not sure," Juli returned, smiling. "Shall we go ask her?"

"Or Thorne," Brian said with a suggestive movement of his eyebrows. "I'm sure he knows."

That was probably true, Juli thought with an odd little hollow feeling inside as she watched the two of them together. Nicole was introducing Thorne to someone now, her arm still holding his. They might be waiting for a decent interval to pass before marrying, Juli thought cynically, but she doubted if they had bothered to observe such proprieties before establishing — or re-establishing — an intimate relationship.

"It's kind of ridiculous, isn't it?" Brian

said scornfully. "All the company executives coming out here and trying to prove how common and ordinary they are one day a year. That's my boss, Dr. Johnson, over there with the big apron. And look at Nicole Taylor! She looks like some oversexed adolescent."

"Thorne doesn't seem to mind," Juli observed wryly.

"I think company management and owners should maintain a little dignity," Brian said.

Juli halfway agreed with his remarks as far as Nicole and her strategically placed heart-shaped appliqués were concerned, but she couldn't resist a teasing. "When you're a company owner, I'm sure you'll never be accused of being undignified."

The remark earned her a slightly sheepish grin from Brian. "I guess I do sound like kind of a stuffed shirt, don't I?" They both laughed and he reached for her hand. "C'mon, let's get something to drink."

They turned toward the refreshment stand, and it was just at that moment that Juli glanced up and met Thorne's eyes. She was separated from him by the barbecue pit and several tables, and yet even at that distance his shock at seeing her was obvious. He evidently got another jolt when he realized she was with Brian, and his chiseled lips compressed into a single hard line.

Juli's eyes dropped first, breaking the electric jolt that had momentarily arced between them. "Maybe I shouldn't have come here," she said uneasily. Somehow she wouldn't put it past Thorne to stride over and arbitrarily demand that she leave. "If the barbecue is supposed to be just for employees —"

"The announcement invited employees, families, and guests," Brian said unconcernedly. He had missed the brief byplay between Juli and Thorne. "Here, what would you like to drink? Coke? Lemonade? Beer?"

Juli chose a lemonade and they made their way to a small, unoccupied table and bench off by themselves. She surreptitiously glanced Thorne's way again, but she needn't have been so careful. His back was to her. Perhaps deliberately, she thought. Then she scoffed at that thought. She was attaching too much importance to herself. He no doubt had been surprised to see her here, but she was just another mouth to feed.

Still, she had to talk to him sometime,

she thought uneasily, though at the moment it looked as if Nicole had a death grip on his arm again. She thought about simply stepping up and politely saying she must speak to him alone for a moment, but she knew she hadn't the nerve for that. She would just have to watch and wait for a chance to catch him alone.

A small pavilion had been set up near the band, and now some square-dancers were performing. Juli and Brian strolled over to watch, carrying their drinks with them. The dancers seemed to be having a good time, the women's full skirts swirling and the men giving an occasional whoop and holler. Later Juli and Brian leaned on the corral fence and watched the children and even a few adults playing more games on horseback, racing at breakneck speed around poles or barrels. A haze of dust hung over the corral, but no one seemed to mind.

Brian introduced her to people here and there, and they finally sat down with two couples he seemed to know fairly well. The men immediately started talking shop, and then a small boy raced up to tell his mother that he'd just won a baseball mitt in some children's contest. He accidentally knocked over what was left of Juli's lemonade.

"Oh, that's all right," Juli said to the boy's apologetic mother. "All that was left was melting ice cubes." Her hands felt sticky, however, and she excused herself to find a faucet to rinse them off.

She was surprised to find comfortable rest rooms built on the far side of the cottonwoods. Thorne didn't skimp on details. She washed her hands and then ran a comb through her hair. Her tan had deepened over the last week and her hair had lightened with flattering sun streaks. She might not be suitably dressed for this occasion, but she had been aware of more than a few complimentary glances. Not from Thorne, however, she thought wryly.

She picked up her purse and went outside again. The trail back to the tables led through the cottonwood grove. She caught her breath as a tall figure stepped out to intercept her.

"What are you doing here with Eames?" he demanded without preliminaries.

"He invited me," Juli stated defiantly. How had Thorne happened to be standing alongside the trail just at the moment she passed by? she wondered warily. Unlikely as it seemed, it almost appeared he had deliberately arranged to catch her alone. In any case, Juli thought as she took a deep, steadying breath, it gave her the opportunity to return his "gift."

Thorne's eyes narrowed, as if he considered her reply too flippant. "And just how do you happen to know him?" he pursued. He had moved up closer to her now and the faint aroma of smoke from the barbecue clung to him. Somehow it only emphasized his rugged masculinity.

Juli retreated a step, determined not to be affected by the man-woman awareness that always seemed to vibrate between them, even in moments of anger. "I . . . I don't think that is any of your concern." Without taking her eyes off him, she fumbled in her purse and fished out the one-hundred-dollar bill. She thrust it at him. "And you can have this back! You have a rather exaggerated idea of the cost of my blouse."

"I presumed there was some mental stress and strain which should be compensated for, as well as the purchase of a new blouse." His voice was contemptuous when he added, "However, I doubt if that was the case. I don't think that you were exactly suffering."

Juli gasped both at the contempt in his voice and the insolence of his words. How dare he be contemptuous of her after what *he* had done! How dare he imply that she had enjoyed his savage attack! And then to think he could send her *money* to compensate for what he had done!

"You tore my blouse off and you have the nerve to —" Words failed Juli in her fury.

"I didn't, as you say, tear your blouse off," he replied with infuriating reasonableness. "I merely ripped the neckline by accident."

"Accident?" echoed Juli.

"By accident," he repeated. He smiled grimly. "If I had intended to tear your blouse off, I would have done a considerably more thorough job of it than that. And I might not have stopped with your blouse," he added with an insinuating glance at the shadowy hollow between her breasts revealed by the deep neckline of the coral dress.

Juli felt her face flame to match the color of the dress, but she managed to retort, "Don't you think Mrs. Taylor might have heard my screams if you had tried that?"

He tilted an eyebrow, his eyes unexpectedly gleaming with wicked amusement. "Would you have screamed? You weren't exactly screaming a moment earlier when —"

"I think you . . . you are despicable!" Juli

gasped. She looked at the hundred-dollar bill in her hand, wondering frantically what to do with it. He had folded his arms against his chest, refusing to take the bill from her outstretched hand. "And I don't want your money!" she cried.

She stepped forward, meaning to stuff the money between his folded arms and muscled chest, but he moved and the green bill fluttered to the ground. He ignored it. A woman and several children came down the trail just then. He touched Juli's arm lightly to make room for the woman to pass. When she resisted, his grip tightened warningly. Rather than make an embarrassing scene, Juli let herself be guided off to one side while he, the benevolent employer, smiled at the kids. The hundred-dollar bill remained where it had settled on the sandy ground.

"You ran into Nikki at the house that day, didn't you?" he mused. "Did you think she was my wife?" His lips twitched as if he found that thought amusing.

"She gave me that impression, yes," Juli agreed with a lift of her head and a futile attempt to control the flush that stormed to her cheeks again. It did not escape her attention that he used a familiar, almost endearing form of Nicole's name. "From what I hear, she soon will be."

"You shouldn't believe every rumor you hear about what may happen," he re-marked lazily. He leaned back against a cottonwood, his long, lean-hipped body re-laxed, yet ready. The fine, bronzed hairs on his forearms glinted against the green com-pany T-shirt. Did he mean, she wondered warily, that nothing definite was yet de-cided between himself and Nicole?

"The rumors aren't only about what may happen, but also what has already happened in the past," Juli finally said tartly.

"Such as?" he challenged.

She bit her lip. She had forgotten his dis-concerting habit of coming bluntly to the point, of refusing to let oblique remarks pass by unchallenged. She had no intention of discussing his past, or present, affair with Nicole, however.

"If you'll excuse me, I believe Brian is waiting for me," Juli said, snapping her purse shut decisively. "You'll find your money on the ground over there."

"It isn't my money," he pointed out, not even glancing toward the bill on the ground. "I sent it to you. Along with the flowers. I trust you enjoyed the long-stemmed roses?"

"Yes, of course, they were beautiful," Juli said, flustered. "Thank you. But I won't take the money. Now, if you'll excuse me, Brian —"

"Let Brian wait," he said insolently. "Patience is one of the virtues of a good researcher."

Juli gasped. "I have consideration for others, even if you do not!"

"Meaning?" He raised a taunting eyebrow.

"Why didn't you open the gates when you first saw I intended leaving, instead of waiting until I almost ran into them?"

"As far as I was concerned, our . . . uh . . . discussion was not yet over. I thought you would come to a sensible stop when you saw the gates were still closed." With a wry twist of his lips, he added, "I didn't realize you were stubborn and hard-headed enough to ram them head on."

Juli caught her breath. He evidently did not realize that in her agitated condition she had actually forgotten the gates were closed, that she had been watching for him and hadn't realized the gates still barricaded her way until she was almost upon them. He really thought she was headstrong enough to ram right into them!

"Of course, it was a bluff," he said,

eyeing her reflectively with those gray-green eyes that reflected the desert coloring around them.

"And yet you couldn't take the chance," Juli taunted, "so you'll never know for sure." She was not about to tell him of the pure terror that had engulfed her when she saw those iron gates barring her way, that thoughts either of ramming or bluffing had never entered her head!

He stepped closer to her, panther-quick in his movements, his folded arms instantly ready at his sides. "If I were you," he suggested softly, "I would not try to bluff *me* very often."

Juli tried to retreat, but something sticky against her back blocked her way. "Wh-what more did you think there was to add to our conversation?" she asked. The words came out shaky, instead of cool and defiant, as she had intended. There was something both menacing and tantalizing in the depths of those gray-green eyes.

"Perhaps it wasn't verbal conversation I had in mind," he murmured. He lifted a tanned hand and touched her lightly, lingeringly, under the chin.

The touch sent the clashing sensations of a cold shiver down her spine and a hot flood through her body. She wanted to slap his hand away, and yet she couldn't seem to move. His fingers trailed down her throat, stroked the nape of her neck, lightly caressed the lobe of her ear.

"What did you have in mind — seducing me into forgetting what you had done to my aunt?" Juli asked scornfully, willing herself not to acknowledge or reveal the wild response surging through her. She held her body rigid, damp hands clenching her purse.

"You consider a kiss in broad daylight seduction? Oh, come now, Juli," he chided, "I don't think you're that innocent."

"I have no intention of discussing my . . . my innocence with you," Juli said. His touch was wildly distracting. She wasn't sure the words even came out coherently. Like some wild animal caught in a trap, she jerked away to escape the trap of his eyes and touch.

The mesmerizing spell snapped, but he didn't let her go. He grabbed her roughly by the arm.

"I intended to come over, flowers in hand, and apologize," he said grimly. "I figured you really were damned upset and I couldn't blame you. But when I went to the florist's shop, there you were standing on the street corner, all dressed up, smiling and talking to some guy as if you hadn't a care in the world. I suppose it was Eames you were with, wasn't it?"

"I wasn't *with* him —"

"Oh, no? I waited by your car for a while, and when you didn't come back I went looking for you. I presume you noticed me when I saw you in that bar. Or maybe you didn't, you were so busy drinking and laughing and letting him get an eyeful of you in that dress."

"It wasn't that way at all!" Juli gasped.

"And here I'd been worried about what I'd done and how upset you were," he said contemptuously. "That was when I realized you'd probably rather have the money than any apology from me. Money seems to be what you consider most important."

Juli stared at him, horrified and sickened at the way he made it all sound so cheap and tawdry. His biting fingers suddenly released her and she staggered slightly.

"But let me give you one little piece of advice. Stay away from Brian Eames," he warned.

"Why? And what gives you the right to give me advice about Brian or . . . or anything else?" she demanded.

"Because —" He hesitated almost imperceptibly, eyes narrowing. "Because he's ambitious and self-centered, and you'll wind up getting hurt."

"I don't see anything wrong with ambition," Juli said defiantly. That tiny moment of hesitation puzzled her, and so did his rather petty criticism of Brian. Then she realized what it must mean. "And that isn't the *real* reason you don't want me around Brian!"

"No?"

"You don't want me around Brian because you're afraid I might find out something you don't want me to know! Something about David. Something that will prove —"

His lean jaw tightened. "Don't be ridiculous."

He broke off as a slim figure in a well-filled-out green T-shirt came toward them. "Thorne, there you are. Where have you been? I've been looking all over for you." Nicole didn't see Juli until Thorne moved to one side. She stopped short, then stepped up to take a firmly possessive grip on Thorne's arm. "I hope I'm not interrupting anything."

Thorne introduced the two women smoothly, without a trace of embarrassment or awkwardness. "Or perhaps you've already met?" he added pleasantly.

At that moment Nicole's dark eyes suddenly widened with recognition. Juli felt a certain grim satisfaction that today she did not look like some waif desperately in need of a job.

"Yes, of course," Nicole agreed coolly. "You came by the house looking for Thorne a few days ago." She glanced up at him, a hint of a frown wrinkling her flawless skin. "I see you found him."

"Yes," Juli agreed. "And we've taken care of our business. So if you'll excuse me?"

"Yes, certainly. It was nice meeting you," Nicole said in the impersonal tone of a person making a polite remark to someone she never expects to see again. She turned back to Thorne, dismissing Juli. "It's time to start serving the food. And there's our announcement to make, too, of course."

Announcement. Juli stumbled away. So, in spite of Thorne's mocking comment about not believing rumors, they were going to announce their engagement today. Her throat suddenly felt dry. Somehow she felt as if he had made a fool of her. Again. But she wouldn't let it show. She wouldn't! She held her back rigid, her hands clenched on her purse. And somehow she managed to walk contemptuously across that hundred-dollar bill without so much as a downward glance.

Chapter Six

Juli and Brian stood in the long line of people that stretched from the serving table into the driveway. Up ahead the company executives were lined up on the opposite side of the table. It was company tradition, Brian said in his usual half-amused, half-disparaging tone, that on this day the executives served the other employees first and ate last themselves. Brian's boss, Dr. Johnson, flourished a large ladle as he prepared to dish up chili. Brian pointed out other V.I.P.'s dishing up salads and serving drinks. The two places at the head of the line, near the huge slabs of barbecued beef, were conspicuously empty.

Then Juli spied them, Thorne helping Nicole up the steps of the pavilion near the band, then leaping lithely to the raised floor himself. Nicole slipped her hand through Thorne's arm as someone brought them a microphone. Juli's appetite suddenly vanished, and she tried to steel herself to show no reaction to the announcement that was coming.

Thorne started out by welcoming everyone, telling them how glad he and Nicole were that they had all come. His only regret was that someone important was missing this year, his brother Jason. Then, more briskly, he added, "Now we have an important announcement to make, one I'm sure you'll all be pleased to hear."

All but one, Juli thought bleakly. She refused to examine why it should matter so much to her that Thorne and Nicole were getting married. Outside of that volatile physical electricity that arced between them, there was certainly nothing between herself and this man talking with such assured self-confidence over the microphone. She only knew that somehow it *did* matter, that her hands felt damp and her throat dry.

"In less than a week, we'll be breaking ground to start building on the next stage of the company's planned expansion program!"

Thorne sounded pleased and almost excited and the crowd applauded, but Juli just stared in astonishment until Brian prodded her to move with the line. Thorne and Nicole weren't announcing their engagement; they were just announcing the start of a new company building program!

Juli's appetite surged back and she loaded her plate with potato and macaroni salads, tiny cherry tomatoes, sliced cucumbers, carrot sticks, and tortilla chips, plus a chunk of crispy Indian fry bread, and a big bowl of chili topped with shredded cheese. Brian looked a little astonished and made some laughing comment about wondering how she kept her gorgeous figure if she always ate like that. Juli just laughed back, feeling oddly light-hearted and giddy. The giddy feeling turned to shakiness when she came to Nicole and Thorne, handing out generous slices of beef expertly carved by Thorne.

Nicole's smooth brow creased ever so slightly in a frown when she saw Juli, but she said nothing. Thorne made some impersonal remark about hoping she enjoyed her meal, much the same as he was saying to everyone. Juli was uncertain whether she was relieved or disappointed, but in any case she thoroughly enjoyed the excellent food. Afterward, they went back for cherry pie and ice cream, plus a piece of genuine cactus candy. It tasted a little like her grandmother's old-fashioned watermelon preserves.

By the time Brian took her home, Juli was tired and a bit bemused by the day's events. What was the relationship between Thorne and Nicole? They were more than business associates, that much seemed obvious, and yet . . .

And yet, what difference did it make one way or the other? Juli chided herself over the next few days. It didn't change the things Thorne had done, his suspicious offer of payment to Aunt Kate, the "accidental" ripping of Juli's blouse, his arrogant suggestion that she would rather have money than an apology. And then warning her to stay away from Brian! He made her furious, and yet even in the midst of that fury she was all too apt to find herself reacting to his virile presence, melting under his touch. With an oddly hollow feeling inside, she realized she quite likely would never see him again.

The real estate agent brought a prospective buyer out Tuesday. Juli continued to clean and sort through David's things. She took a big pile of books to a second-hand store, books on subjects ranging from electronics to geology, Arizona history to Indian lore. On Thursday she decided to open up the hide-a-bed in the living room and vacuum the mattress. To her surprise she found there was no mattress inside, just a folded blanket. When she lifted the blanket, papers fluttered everywhere, pages and pages of notes and diagrams and maps. One map appeared to be on old parchment, the lines faded, the paper folded and refolded so many times that a brittle piece of it broke off in her hand.

Juli looked at the papers, bewildered. Why had David hidden them in the sofa? Because they were hidden, there was no doubt about that. This was not just another of David's haphazard piles of old junk.

Some of the notes were on quite technical geological subjects. Others were numbered in reference to corresponding numbers on various maps, most of which looked like copies of the parchment map. There was a page of dates and figures that appeared to show times of sunrise and sunset at various times of the year. And there were pages and pages of rambling notes in which David seemed to have been more or less talking to himself on paper, putting forth various theories about the location of something.

And then a few shocking words and phrases leaped out of the notes at her. David saying to himself that he doubted if this problem had ever been approached on a really scientific basis before, that he was certain he had achieved a real scientific breakthrough by correlating geological, historical, and personal investigative data. *Scientific breakthrough.*

This was what David had been working on, Juli realized with a sense of shock. Not some electronic invention or development, either on his own or for the company, but *this.* And what, exactly, was this?

Juli sank into a chair and studied the papers again. She finally figured out that David had been searching for a mine, a gold mine that he referred to as the Lost Dutchman's Mine, that had been lost for many years. He had, she also realized, evidently paid someone a rather large amount of money for the old map. The mine was somewhere in the Superstition Mountains. The name jarred her. That was where Jason Taylor had slipped and fallen to his death! Could David have had something to do with that death? Juli wondered in horror.

With shaky relief she read on as David talked to himself about Jason's death, his scorn coming through as he said Jason was searching in the wrong area entirely, an area David himself had never been near. *Perhaps the accident serves him right, however, for going behind my back and cheating on our previous agreement,* David had written. David sounded callous and certainly evidenced no great regret over Jason's death, but neither did he sound involved or responsible. With a jolt Juli remembered something Brian had told her, that Jason Taylor's hobby was looking for old mines. So it wasn't Thorne and Taylor Electronics whom David thought had cheated him in the past, she realized. It was Jason Taylor.

Stunned and incredulous, Juli gathered the papers into a neat stack. Whatever had gotten into David to let his work at the company suffer while he chased after some lost gold mine? It was incredible, so unlike what she thought she knew of David, and yet it was all there for her to see. It explained the collections of rocks he had piled all over the place, rocks he evidently thought had some geological significance in relation to the gold. It explained his absences from work, because he was out looking for the gold mine when he should have been on the job. Juli just stood there, shocked and stunned.

And then another thought that was almost as shocking and dismaying as what she had just discovered struck her. *She owed Thorne an apology.* She had been wrong, dead wrong in thinking Taylor

Electronics had done anything to cheat David or Aunt Kate. She had been wrong in her beliefs, wrong in her accusations, wrong in her actions.

But she couldn't go crawling to him, apologetically begging for his forgiveness. Empty as the thought of never seeing him again had left her, she couldn't humble herself before his scornful, knowing eyes, his inevitable taunting: "I told you so." She just couldn't! All that day and the next she tried to avoid the responsibility of going to him and admitting she was wrong, tried to rationalize and argue her way out of it. She squirmed and wiggled and tried to escape it, but finally her basic sense of justice and responsibility impaled her.

She put it off until Saturday morning and then finally, reluctantly, dressed in mint-green slacks and white tank top, she started out. She parked her car and walked toward the front door of the Taylor house, dreading what she had to do, apprehensive that she might encounter Nicole again, and yet deep down feeling a tremble of excited anticipation at seeing Thorne. She was halfway up the walkway when the sound of her own name spoken by a commanding male voice startled her.

"Oh! You . . . you surprised me."

Thorne was standing at the half-open gate in the high wall that concealed the pool. He was wearing only brief, navy swim trunks and a white towel slung around his neck. Drops of water glittered on his tanned skin and glistened in his bronzed hair. He looked poised, predatory, again the pagan sun-devil with mocking eyes she had encountered on the ridge.

"I . . . There was something I wanted to talk to you about," Juli faltered.

He swung the gate open wider in a gesture that was more acquiescing than inviting. She brushed by him, carefully avoiding contact, clutching her sheaf of papers. He motioned her toward a cushioned redwood chair and settled in a matching chaise longue himself, leanly muscled legs casually crossed at the ankles.

"Is . . . is Nicole around?" Juli asked, annoyed with herself for asking, but needing to know.

His lips twitched in a slight movement that might have indicated amusement at her concern or annoyance at her temerity for asking such a question. "No, she went back to Scottsdale. She and my mother should be coming down together in a few days."

"Oh." It all sounded so intimate, as if

143

they were already a family. Determinedly, she put those thoughts out of her mind. They had nothing to do with why she was here today. She took a deep breath. "I have come to apologize to you. I have learned that what David thought was a 'scientific breakthrough' had nothing to do with electronics or your company, and I was wrong in making demands and accusations." She thrust the sheaf of papers at him.

Eyebrows lifted quizzically, Thorne took the papers. He started to rifle through them, straightened up in the lounge chair, and examined each with attentive care. For long minutes he said nothing. Juli looked around restlessly, appreciating again the way the pool had been built to blend artfully with the surroundings, almost as if it were a natural oasis among the desert boulders. The patio provided cool shade, with green plants in hanging pots giving a lush, garden atmosphere that contrasted with the desert saguaro and prickly pear on the far side of the pool. The gracefully leaning palm added a final touch of elegance. The morning sun felt pleasant on her rigid back, but did nothing to relax her tense nerves.

Finally Thorne whistled softly. "So that was it," he murmured. "I'll be damned.

This is why David was so preoccupied and secretive. People speculated about everything from alcohol to gambling or women, and all the time he had gold fever."

"Gold fever?" Juli repeated doubtfully.

Thorne leaned back, the papers resting on his sun-darkened thighs, gray-green eyes reflective. "It's hard for someone like you or me to understand, I suppose, how some people can develop this obsession, this fever to search for gold. But you have only to look back at the California and Alaska gold rushes to see how it infected some people. Perhaps an addiction to gambling would be the closest comparison. A person feels sure that with the next throw of the dice, or the next turn of the shovel, he'll strike it rich. There's an old saying that you're better off getting struck by a rattlesnake than bit by the gold bug."

"But it seems so . . . so incredible, so unbelievable," Juli protested. "David was so intelligent. And he never seemed to care all that much about material things or riches."

Thorne nodded. "But gold fever can make fools out of the most intelligent of men. Gold seems to hold a fascination that has nothing to do with feelings about other material luxuries." He looked at the old, worn map again. "It's not all that unusual for an otherwise level-headed man to get hooked on looking for the Lost Dutchman's Mine. And quite a few have lost their lives in the search."

"Including your brother?" she asked tentatively.

Thorne took a sip from a tall glass resting on the low redwood table between them. He lifted the glass in a questioning gesture, but she shook her head. "Including Jason," he agreed finally. "I always thought looking for the Lost Dutchman and some other mines was just a hobby with Jason, but perhaps it wasn't. Perhaps he had gold fever, too. I knew he and David seemed friendly for a while, and then they were hardly on speaking terms. I didn't give it much thought at the time, but evidently it had something to do with this."

"It's still so hard to understand," Juli said helplessly.

He swung lean legs over the edge of the lounge chair. "A world-famous author once headed an expedition to look for the Lost Dutchman. A whole group of people spent months climbing around on Weaver's Needle with ropes and nets in some wild scheme. People do strange things where gold is concerned. Some skeletons have been found in the Superstitions with the skull separated from the other bones, as if the victim had been beheaded. Some call it the Dutchman's Curse."

Juli shuddered involuntarily, and Thorne smiled — a smile that for once seemed more genuine and sympathetic than mocking.

"Of course, there are other less fanciful explanations than that of some mysterious curse. The people could have died of natural causes, such as thirst or heat, and the bones been scattered by animals. But if the danger of the curse isn't real, the danger of someone inexperienced dying of heat or thirst in the interior of the Superstitions is quite real. There are still a few old prospectors living back in there looking for the gold, though."

Juli shook her head, still bewildered by all this. "This changes everything, of course. You don't owe Aunt Kate anything, and you won't have to pay."

He shrugged. "This doesn't change anything with regards to your aunt. As I believe I pointed out to you earlier, I have known all along that David did not make some invention or discovery of great value to the company." His voice was lightly mocking, but the tone was more teasing than derisive.

"Then why are you giving her the money?"

"Various reasons. Giving a payment directly to Mrs. Flynn could be cheaper and less bothersome than a long, drawn-out court case. Also, having a sweet little old lady sue the company for fraud or something equally damning would not be very good publicity."

He spoke easily, almost carelessly, but he didn't meet Juli's eyes, and suddenly Juli suspected why. He didn't want to admit it, but Aunt Kate's plight had touched a soft place in his heart, a soft place that until this moment she would not even have guessed existed.

"Frankly, I thought your story about David's mother was just a phony sob story, part of your scheme to con money out of the company," he admitted. "But we ran a fast check and found out you were telling the truth — at least on that point."

His emphasis did not escape her. She toyed uneasily with the strap of her purse, her head bent forward so her soft hair fell partway across her face. "I'm sorry. But I honestly believed everything I said about David doing something big and important for the company."

"I know."

She stood up and he rose to his feet, also. He was barefoot and she in high-heeled sandals, but even so, he towered over her. He handed the papers back to her. The fragile parchment map was almost in pieces by now.

"It still seems too incredible. The map looks old and authentic, and I think David paid someone a fair amount of money for it." She hesitated. "I wonder . . . I mean, isn't it just *possible* —"

"Look, don't *you* go getting gold fever, too," he warned. "There might be ten thousand 'old and authentic' Lost Dutchman maps floating around, and there's always someone willing to sell one to a sucker who is willing to buy."

Juli smiled. "I suppose so." She moved toward the gate, acutely aware of his almost-naked body beside her and the easy grace of his barefoot stride.

"But you're still not totally convinced, are you?" he suggested.

"It still seems hard to believe David would go off on a completely wild-goose chase," she admitted.

"How would you like to hike into the Superstitions yourself?" he said unexpectedly. "See the place for yourself and see how much chance *you* think there is of finding any lost gold mine there."

Juli looked up at him in surprise, her

heart suddenly hammering erratically.

"How about tomorrow? It's Sunday. We'll take a lunch and make a day of it." His smile was friendly, his eyes smoky-warm.

Juli was never quite sure what was said next, but somehow it was all arranged. He would pick her up at the trailer Sunday morning. He would bring the lunch. She should wear heavy shoes suitable for hiking, not flimsy sandals. This last was said without criticism, however, as Thorne cast an appreciative glance at her slim ankles and high heels.

Somehow, Juli got through the day. She laughed at herself when she was almost too excited to eat supper. She was acting like some giddy adolescent going on her first date! And yet she did have the heady feeling of being on the edge of a very special first in her life, the first time she had ever really been in love.

She prepared for bed early, telling herself she needed to get a good night's sleep, but somehow doubtful that she would be able to sleep at all. She showered and washed her hair and was just laying out her clothes for the next day when the lights, without so much as a flicker of warning, blinked out.

She sat there in the darkness waiting for

them to come on again, but nothing happened. She peered outside, but since no other residences were visible from the trailer, it was impossible to tell whether the electricity was out all over or just at the trailer. She felt her way down the length of the trailer to the living room and peered out again. There was no moon. The boulder-strewn ridge was a dark blot against the starry sky.

She hesitated uncertainly. Of course, she was ready for bed, and once asleep it wouldn't matter if the electricity was on or off. But she found the idea of waking up in the night and not knowing the comforting reassurance of being able to snap on a light unsettling. Resolutely, she found a flashlight in a drawer, slipped on a robe, and went outside to the electrical box fastened to a post. Perhaps a fuse had blown.

She opened the electrical box. There were several switches inside. Tentatively, she flipped them back and forth, glancing hopefully at the trailer as she did so, but nothing happened. She tried again. Suddenly the lights blinked on and off several times, finally settling to a reassuring glow. Juli didn't know if she had done something right, or if the power company had done something to correct a general electric outage, but she was relieved.

In the morning Juli had only time to dress and fix a quick breakfast before Thorne arrived in an old four-wheel-drive pickup. He seemed in a marvelous, almost playful mood. He voiced approval of her hiking shoes, but his eyes gleamed with even more appreciative approval of her hip-molding jeans. Juli fought down a breathless giddiness. This was just a Sunday hike, nothing more.

The front seat of the pickup was crowded with picnic basket, backpack, and insulated water jug. Juli was squeezed up against Thorne by the time they were inside and ready to go, her leg pressed with almost embarrassing intimacy against his lean thigh. Though he didn't seem to object!

They took a shortcut on the old highway that led directly across the dry riverbed without benefit of a bridge. The ever-present creosote bush grew in clumps on the dry bottom, though the mesquite and palo verde trees clustered along the sandy banks. Tracks where cars had squirreled around in the sand crisscrossed the area.

The drive up to the Superstitions was

pleasant, the talk casual but friendly. Juli had a hard time concentrating with Thorne's arm brushing against her whenever he turned the steering wheel and the hard length of his leg pressed against hers. Long before they reached the dirt road that led to the south entrance of the Superstitions Wilderness area, Juli could see the massive battlements of the western tip of the mountains rising abruptly from the desert floor. The cliffs were straight up and down and yet convoluted into strange, tortured shapes, massive and barren, brooding and majestic.

The bumpy, dusty road led through saguaro and mesquite, palo verde and ocotillo. They finally parked in a rocky, sloping area with several other cars. Juli could only stare in awe. Stretching off to the left was a sheer, rose-colored wall. The trail led up a steep canyon jumbled with boulders and cactus, overlooked by incredibly shaped and balanced rocks on either side. A cave was visible far up on one side, seemingly impregnable above a rounded wall of yellow-green rock. It was all rough and wild and incredibly beautiful.

Thorne efficiently packed the lunch in his backpack and shrugged the metal frame over his shoulders. Water gurgled in the stream that trickled down the canyon, but he added a filled canteen to the pack. With a smile he said Juli would probably have all she could do to make the climb up the trail to Fremont Saddle without any additional weight.

Juli hesitated. "Is it dangerous?" she asked doubtfully.

He shook his head negatively. "Not if you use common sense and stay on the trail. Lots of people hike as far as we're going today. Actually, we're just on the edge of the wilderness area. And it definitely can be dangerous back in the interior, off the beaten trails, especially in the hotter, dryer months."

The edge of the Superstitions was wild enough for her, Juli thought as they started up the well-worn trail, and the view grew more awesome the farther they went. The rocks above the canyon trail were an incredible mixture of the graceful and grotesque. There were spires and turrets, columns and knobs and domes that to her imagination were fairy castles one moment, medieval fortresses the next. Some rocks had the shape of Impressionistic, elongated human figures, forever trapped in stone; others were grotesque distortions of some demon animal world, nightmare figures of a tortured dream. In places one immense boulder balanced atop another, as if some giant had marked his trail with piled rocks.

Thorne let Juli scramble along by herself, seldom offering a helping hand, though they paused often to rest. The trail crossed and re-crossed the creek, plentiful with running water at this time of year, though Thorne said it dwindled to stagnant pools later on.

Thorne seemed relaxed, almost jovial, full of interesting little bits of information. He showed Juli a tiny cactus wren's nest tucked right in among the needle-sharp cholla spines, at first glance a dangerously unlikely spot for a nest, but a safe refuge from the tiny bird's enemies. He pointed out how the tall saguaro cactuses, with their twisted arms, looked fat and healthy now because rain had been plentiful this season. In dry times the leathery, pleated skin folded up like an accordion as water was used up.

"Somewhere I read that you can cut the top off some cactuses and find water inside," Juli said.

"The barrel cactus," he agreed, pointing out one of the round, stubby plants that fit its name. He laughed. "However, some writers make it sound as if all you have to do is cut off the top and dip out buckets of fresh water. Actually, what is inside is just a wet pulp and tastes terrible. But I suppose it could save your life if you were dying of thirst."

"I'm not dying of thirst, but I certainly could use a drink," Juli admitted.

Thorne slipped the pack from his back and offered her the canteen. She found drinking from the container awkward, but managed a few sips. Thorne took a long, experienced gulp. He sat on a flat-topped rock and made room for her beside him. "What do you think now about finding a lost gold mine here?" he inquired.

Juli laughed and shook her head ruefully. "It would be easier to find the proverbial needle in a haystack. Such strange rocks," she murmured. "Almost like strange, sad beings standing there waiting for release."

Thorne's gaze followed hers to the vertical stones clustered together on the far side of the canyon. "One old Indian legend says that once there was a great flood and the people came to the mountains to escape it. Their god said they would be saved if not a word was spoken until the floodwaters receded. But one person did speak — a squaw, no doubt," he interjected with a teasing smile, "and the entire tribe was turned to stone and you see them there now."

"I halfway believe it," Juli said tremulously. "It seems like a place where anything could happen. Was it around here that Jason . . ." Her voice trailed off awkwardly.

"It was some distance from here where he fell, on the other side of Weaver's Needle," Thorne said quietly.

"Do you think there is gold here?" Juli asked slowly.

"In general, most geologists say no, it isn't here. But others say volcanic action could have pushed up a vertical vein of gold-bearing rose quartz, usually called a chimney lode, from deep in the earth. Some big mining companies are supposed to have investigated in the past and decided the area was worthless. I think the theory of most of those who search here is simply that gold is where you find it."

"But what do *you* think?" Juli persisted, eyeing his strong, lean profile.

"I'm no geologist or treasure hunter." He looked at her and grinned, then gazed off toward the mouth of the canyon where desert and barren mountains rolled endlessly to the horizon. His voice was a little husky when he spoke, revealing how much he loved this brutal, yet beautiful, land. "I think the real treasure here is just what you see — the rocks and cactuses and desert and sky and freedom."

Juli drew her knees up and rested her arms and chin on them. "What is the story of the lost mine? What makes so many people believe so strongly that it is here that they risk their lives searching for it?"

He leaned back against another rock. "There are so many stories that they become confusing. Some say that the Apaches had gold here — a sacred, hidden cache. A Spanish family from Mexico, the Peraltas, for whom this canyon is named, is reputed to have taken out a fortune in gold in the early 1800s. The Lost Dutchman tale started later on when a man named Jacob Waltz showed up in Phoenix with gold and was thought to come back here to get more whenever his supply ran out. On his deathbed he gave a woman friend and her son instructions on how to find his mine and they spent years searching but never found anything. And a lot of others have searched ever since. There's something about the Superstitions that seems to capture the imagination."

"But it seems, with all who have looked,

that something would have been found if it were really here," Juli mused.

"There are various theories on that, too. One is that the Indians didn't like whites prowling around their sacred mountains and filled in the pit of the mine. Another is that an earthquake in the late 1800s changed and concealed everything. And another is that if anyone gets too close to finding the treasure, the Dutchman's Curse does him in, of course."

Juli glanced around, her uneasiness only half-pretended. "I hope the Lost Dutchman doesn't think we're after his gold!"

"Do you remember that in David's papers there was a schedule showing sunrise times?" Thorne asked suddenly, and Juli nodded. "One of the stories says old Waltz said that on a particular day of the year the first rays of the rising sun shone through a 'window' in a rock and struck his mine."

"Poor David," Juli murmured. Had he really believed that somewhere in this wild and desolate land he could pinpoint one small area of gold?

Thorne nodded. "I guess he never heard the other story that says the afternoon sun shines into the mine."

"You don't believe any of the stories?"

Thorne hesitated. "No, not really. And

yet . . ." His voice trailed off and he looked toward the saddle at the head of the canyon toward which they were climbing. He stood up and reached for the pack. "I can vouch for the fact that years ago someone took a shot at me when I was poking around La Barge Canyon. As I've said, gold fever does strange things to otherwise sensible people."

They started off again, passing an older couple with walking sticks gamely plodding up the trail. They met an exuberant group of Boy Scouts returning from an overnight camping outing. As they neared the rim of Fremont Saddle, Juli felt a tingle of excited anticipation. What lay on the other side? She could understand how the frontier explorers kept pushing on, that one more ridge always beckoned with an irresistible pull.

A surprisingly cool, brisk breeze picked up as they neared the top, and Thorne slipped his arm around Juli's shoulders. They climbed the last few steps together and Juli's breath caught at the vista that lay sprawled before them. It was almost frightening in its desolation, and yet strangely beautiful, too. Dry mountains, craggy rocks, distant walls, and dominating it all the sheer, massive monolith called Weaver's

Needle. It rose dark and somber out of the desert valley, rounded at the tip, too thick and bulky really to resemble a needle, but magnificent against the sky. It looked as if it had stood there forever and would stand there into eternity, aloof and impregnable. Juli suddenly felt very small and insignificant.

"It's supposed to be named for Pauline Weaver, the frontier explorer," Thorne explained.

"A woman?" Juli gasped.

"No. But it makes you wonder if perhaps he became a he-man explorer to escape the curse of that name, doesn't it?" He laughed. His arm was still draped companionably around her shoulders.

Juli looked up at him while he went on talking about eating their lunch here or hiking on down into the valley, but she wasn't really hearing. She was studying the strong lines of his face, seeing the character behind the tanned, handsome features, recognizing a warm, companionable side to his nature that had been hidden before. Today he seemed so much less remote than before, so much more reachable, as if the wall that usually surrounded him had crumbled away. Was it just because of her apology — or was there some deeper reason? He turned her to face him and she was conscious again of his powerful maleness, the hard length of his body, the primitively physical feelings, both tantalizing and frightening, that he aroused in her. But now there was something more, something that she was almost more afraid to face.

Unexpectedly, he tipped her chin up. "You look as if your mind is a million miles away," he chided.

"No, no I'm listening." Her voice was husky. Perhaps, she thought tremulously, it would be safer if her thoughts were a million miles away, away from what she knew was happening to her. It seemed incredible after the way they had fought and argued and accused each other, and yet she knew it had started from the very first moment she met him. Now she was no longer poised on the precipitous edge of being in love. She had fallen, tumbled with reckless abandon like one of those balancing rocks careening headlong into the canyon. She wondered if he could feel the wild throbbing of her heart, a pounding that had nothing to do with the exertion of the climb.

"Do you want to hike into the valley?" he repeated. His fingers caressed her chin while his eyes roamed her face.

Was that all he was asking?

"Yes," she whispered. And then, more fiercely to herself: Yes, *yes* to whatever he asked!

"We should get started, then," he said.

But neither of them made a move toward the trail sloping steeply into the valley. His hand slid behind her neck, and then almost roughly his fingers tangled in her soft hair, forcing her head back while his other arm molded her body against his. His demanding mouth conquered hers without resistance, the pressure almost painful until a matching passion surged within her and swept away all else. Her arms, seeking to hold him as he was holding her, met the awkward bulk of the backpack and crept instead to caress his thick hair. His mouth moved against hers, commanding, exploring, possessing, dominating her with his strength and virility.

The piercing cry of some hunting bird shrieked overhead as it searched for prey, and some vague thought in the back of Juli's mind warned her that she might also be prey to a powerful predator. But she ignored the warning and recklessly returned his kiss, a willing victim whose arms and lips demanded more.

Chapter Seven

Juli's head rested against Thorne's shoulder as they drove back toward Cholla. Her muscles felt sore and tired, but her mind soared with the joy of the day. They had descended into the valley and eaten their lunch near the base of Weaver's Needle. From beneath, it seemed even more towering and massive, a monumental, indestructible work of nature. They had taken off their shoes, rolled up their pantlegs, and romped in the creek like a couple of children. They splashed each other with water, laughed, and wound up kissing again while the water swirled around their bare legs, its surprising chill unnoticed while the fire of the kiss raged through them. They had stayed as late as they dared, and the sun was a sinking red ball in the west when they finally returned hand in hand to the pickup.

Now Thorne reached over and lightly caressed the tendrils of soft hair on her temple. "Asleep?" he said softly.

"Just dozing," Juli murmured, not wanting him to know she found the pillow of his shoulder too exciting for sleep, even in her present state of weariness.

"We're just coming into Cholla now. Would you like to stop and have dinner somewhere?"

Juli straightened up. She felt grimy and dirty, her clothes anything but fresh after the day's exertions. "I'm afraid they'd toss me out of any respectable place," she admitted. "I could fix something at the trailer, if you wouldn't mind. Perhaps an omelet and salad?"

"Sounds great," he said promptly. "I always wanted a girl who knows how to do something more than read a restaurant menu."

The words echoed rapturously in Juli's ears. *I always wanted a girl* . . . As if she might be that very girl he'd always wanted!

At the trailer Juli excused herself so she could wash up first and get the meal started while he cleaned up. She stripped off the grimy blouse and turned on the hot water in the bathroom. Nothing happened. She twisted and jiggled the faucet doubtfully, then hopefully tried the other faucet. It was equally useless. What in the world was wrong? She remembered there had been only a weak trickle of water that morning, but at the time she had been in too much of a hurry to worry about it. Now there wasn't so much as a drop of water. Reluctantly, she slipped the blouse on again and went out to tell Thorne.

"I'll go have a look in the pump house," he said promptly. "It's probably just some minor thing."

"Oh, you don't need to do that," Juli protested. "I know you're tired and its dirty out there and —"

"And you probably think I'm a company president who doesn't know one end of a pump from the other," he teased. "Someday I'll have to show you the little ranchhouse out in the desert where we lived when I was a boy and milked the cow and fed the chickens." He was already grabbing the flashlight from the kitchen counter and starting outside.

Juli got the salad greens out of the refrigerator. They were already washed, but her hands felt too grimy to touch them. She went into the bathroom again, but the washcloth was too dry and stiff to have any cleansing effect on her hands. Thorne returned in just a few minutes.

He set the flashlight back on the counter. "I think it's an electrical problem."

Juli chewed her lower lip uncertainly. "Something must have happened to the pump when the electricity blinked off and on last night. Or maybe it was something wrong with the pump that made the electricity go off. I don't know anything about electricity or pumps," she added helplessly.

"The power outage was general," he said briefly.

Somehow his voice sounded a little less warm and friendly than it had all day, and Juli mentally cursed the uncooperative pump. Of all times for it to fail! This made such an awkward, disappointing end to an otherwise perfect day. She couldn't even offer him a cup of coffee without water to prepare it.

"I guess I'll have to offer you a raincheck on the meal," she said unhappily.

He stood there eyeing her, an odd expression on his face. She looked at him uncertainly. Surely he wasn't angry over something that wasn't even her fault, was he? Perhaps he was disappointed, she decided hopefully. She knew she certainly was.

He stood there a moment longer, lean and rugged and somehow remote again. Then he seemed to come to a decision. "We'll go to my place. Estelle can whip up something for us to eat. Bring your bathing suit and a change of clothes and we'll take a dip before we eat." His tone was crisp and authoritative, the voice of a man accustomed to giving commands and having them obeyed.

Juli hesitated. She hated the idea of going to bed without so much as a shower to wash the day's grime away, and the thought of a swim was deliciously inviting. But she didn't want Thorne to feel he was somehow obligated to issue this invitation, especially when he seemed so aloof and remote again. "That isn't necessary," she said uneasily. "Besides, it's a little cool for a swim."

"The pool is heated."

Still Juli hesitated, but she knew she didn't want the day to end on this oddly uncomfortable note. "I'll take my car so you won't have to drive me back later."

"Don't be ridiculous," he said. His voice left no room for argument.

She gathered up a bathing suit, a change of clothing, and a few items to refresh her makeup. At his house he suggested she go on out to the bathhouse and change while he talked to Estelle about something to eat. She did as he suggested, finding the bathhouse as luxurious as everything else about the Taylor estate. She showered away the day's grime before slipping into her bathing suit, ruefully wondering why she always felt more daring when purchasing some items of clothing than when wearing them later. The burgundy-colored suit was one piece, but cut so high on the hip and so low in the back that an almost-indecent amount of skin was exposed. She cracked the bathhouse door open, then hurried across the concrete patio and slid into the pool before Thorne arrived. The evening air was cool and the contrast of the heated pool was almost like slipping into bathwater. It enveloped her with delicious warmth, gliding like a sensuous caress around her legs and waist and breasts.

The overhead lights were not turned on now. A single tinted light, concealed somewhere on the far side of the pool, illuminated the palm tree from below. Part of the pool curved around one of the huge boulders, making a private little cove on the far end. It could be a tropical island, Juli thought dreamily as she supported herself against the edge of the pool, her legs moving idly in the smooth water. An island paradise for two . . .

Suddenly she was aware she was not alone and she glanced swiftly behind her to see Thorne standing there in the shadows.

"I didn't hear you! How long have you been standing there?"

"Only a moment." His hands were on his hips, the powerful breadth of his shoulders emphasized by the brevity of the navy trunks stretched across his lean hips. He didn't move, but a flicker of breeze played shadows across the muscles of his chest.

"Aren't you coming in?" Juli asked, somehow uneasy at the way he just stood there motionless, his face shadowed so he could watch her but she could not see his eyes. She had the strange feeling that he was struggling with something within himself. What? Had he not wanted her to come here? Did he feel uncomfortable with her here in the home everyone said he would soon be sharing with Nicole? That thought brought a sudden, painful lurch to Juli's heart. She hadn't thought about Nicole all day. She had been too wrapped up in the wondrous discovery of her own feelings. She doubted that Thorne had thought about Nicole, either. But that had been while they were away from here, and now they were back.

Without warning, Thorne's body arced cleanly into the pool, slicing the water with knifelike precision. He came up on the far side of the pool, ducked under again, and came up beside her, so close she felt the brush of his skin against her body. Now he was grinning, his eyes sparkling with a roguish glitter, his manner completely changed, as if he had undergone some underwater transformation. He ran one hand up the smooth, bare curve of her hip. The intimacy of the gesture both shocked and thrilled her, and his devilish eyes told her he knew it.

"How come you hid yourself in the pool before I got a chance to see you in your bathing suit?" he chided with mock reproach.

"I'm not hiding," she protested, though she knew it wasn't true.

"We don't even have to wear suits, you know, if you'd rather not. Once you try swimming in the nude, you'll never want to wear a suit again."

Juli's lips parted and she stifled a gasp of shock. He laughed, a throaty chuckle, and Juli knew he had said it purposely to shock her. For a moment she thought about recklessly calling his bluff, but the challenge in his eyes made her suddenly afraid it was no bluff. Instead, she dived under the water and swam to the far side of the pool, liking the fresh, clean feel of the water gliding over her skin. But Thorne was too quick for her, and when she came up he was already there, laughing at her. Under the tinted light his skin was copper, his teeth a white flash, and the clinging droplets of water glittered like iridescent jewels on his gleaming skin.

She went underwater again, twisting and turning, laughing delightedly when she managed to elude him. They chased each other back and forth, above and beneath the water, in and out of the secluded cove at the far end of the pool. But Juli's agility was no match for Thorne's speed and power. Just when she thought she had outmaneuvered him, his hand would reach out and capture her ankle or his arm encircle her waist. Once she ducked around and caught him by the leg, but instead of pulling away as she always did, he somersaulted underwater and came up with his arms around her.

"Now who caught whom?" he challenged laughingly.

"I . . . I'm not sure," Juli gasped. "But I have to rest, or you're going to drown me!"

They were in the secluded cove behind the boulder. Here the light was only a dim, reflected glow, the water and Thorne's eyes both darkly mysterious. Juli slipped away to the side of the pool and supported herself with elbows draped behind her as she tried to catch her breath.

He followed, a strong hand on either side of her imprisoning her within the cage of his arms. "If I drown you, it will only be with kisses," he said huskily. His lips showered her wet throat and shoulder with feathery kisses and then moved boldly to the hollow between her breasts.

Juli caught her breath in a gasp, unable to deny the urgent messages the touch of his lips sent racing through every nerve in her body, messages she found shocking and yet almost irresistibly powerful and demanding. She sucked in her breath and plunged straight down to escape his imprisoning arms, but she was too tired and winded to stay under for more than a few moments. When she came up and grabbed the side of the pool, he swam over beside her again.

"Why did you do that?" he asked reproachfully.

She started to make some flippant reply, but the words caught in her throat. The teasing gleam was gone from his eyes now, replaced by something dark and inscrutable. "I . . . I don't know," she said, almost in a whisper.

"Don't you like having me touch you?"

"Yes . . . no . . . oh, I don't know! It does something to me . . ."

"Something you don't like?"

"I don't know," she whispered, but that wasn't true. She liked his touch, liked the feel of his skin and lips and the ripple of his muscles and the brush of his crisp hair, exulted in them even as some more sensible part of her mind sent frantic warning signals.

As they talked some slight motion of the water drifted their bodies closer together, the movement almost imperceptible but somehow inexorable. Like the moth to the flame, she thought tremulously.

Suddenly his legs reached around hers, catching and holding her by the ankles, molding the underwater halves of their bodies together. She could feel the hard male power of his body, and she knew the times she had ducked and escaped him before were only because he let her go, that there was no escaping him now. The water eddied around them, undulating their bodies in motion together. Thorne didn't speak. He just watched her eyes and she was afraid of what they revealed to his experienced gaze.

"What are you thinking?" he demanded softly. Above water there was an almost decent distance between them, but beneath the water he still held her in that inescapable grip.

What was she thinking? Her heart pounded in reply because it wasn't what she was thinking that really seemed important right now; it was what she was feeling in every nerve and muscle of her body. She was feeling dormant, barely acknowledged desires throb to life, desires that were a part of the awakening love she felt for Thorne. And yet there was an uneasy awareness within her that in him those pulsating desires might be quite separate and distinct from love.

"I . . . I was thinking that you seemed so . . . changeable today," she faltered.

"Changeable?" he repeated. He raised an eyebrow, a cool, almost impersonal gesture that seemed at odds with the way their bodies melded intimately together beneath the water.

"I don't know . . ." Juli's voice trailed off helplessly. How could she explain it? All day he had seemed so warmly companionable, lightly teasing, but in an affectionate sort of way. She had felt so at ease with him. His kisses at the mountains had been passionate and demanding, but they were also spontaneous and natural, without guise or calculation. Now his expert caresses seemed deliberately calculated to arouse and challenge her. And in between had been that brief but uncomfortable period of remote withdrawal she sensed in him. Why had he invited her here tonight? Did he have something more than a dip and dinner in mind? She knew he did, and she found the thought both frightening and disturbingly alluring.

"There seem to be a lot of things you 'don't know' tonight," he mocked lightly.

"When do you expect your mother and Nicole to arrive?" she asked, abruptly trying to change the subject.

His eyes narrowed. "In a few days," he answered noncommittally. A forefinger played lightly with the strap of her bathing suit, would have slid it off her shoulder if she had not shrugged it back in place. "Do you really want to talk about my mother and former sister-in-law right now?" he asked, his hand still lightly threatening the stability of the strap.

"Are you afraid to talk about Nicole?" Now it was Juli's turn to challenge.

"Of course not. It's just that there are subjects that are so much more interesting to discuss." His hand moved up to caress her temple, and his voice was a caress, too.

"The way your eyes sparkle. The way your skin feels like satin against my fingertips. The perfume of your hair and the taste of your lips . . ."

His fingers traced the outline of her lips and then his mouth touched hers lightly, like a connoisseur sampling a fine wine. Then the teasing touch deepened to a kiss that sent Juli's senses reeling dizzily, and she would have slipped beneath the water if it were not for the powerful grip of his legs and the arm supporting her. Dimly, from somewhere far off, she heard a voice.

"Someone — someone is calling!" she gasped.

He lifted his dark head, scowling at the interruption.

"Mr. Taylor? Are you still out here? The omelet is almost ready."

"We'll be in in just a moment, thank you," Thorne called back, nothing in his steady voice betraying the pounding heartbeat Juli could feel in his chest, pressed against her own. His caresses might have been deliberately calculated to arouse her, but he had not remained unaffected himself. He released her from the locked grip of his legs and the water surging around her hips felt almost cool now after the heat of his body.

"Saved by the bell — the dinner bell," he said lightly with a mocking smile. Pointedly, he added, "Though there is nothing that says we *must* eat right now."

"Omelets toughen as they cool," Juli said shakily. "We should eat it right away."

"Of course."

He helped her out of the pool, Juli sharply aware of his eyes roaming over the daring bathing suit, and they went to separate rooms to dress. Juli had brought cream-colored slacks and a silky fuchsia blouse. She refreshed her lipstick and eyeshadow, though her hands were so shaky she had to wipe off smeared lipstick once and start again. She knew her honey tan looked better than any artificial makeup she could put on her skin.

Thorne was waiting when she stepped outside and they went into the dining room together. Juli caught her breath. This was no casual snack. The only light came from three slim candles in a silver candelabrum. The soft light flickered on creamy damask tablecloth, fine china, and elegant silverware. A corked bottle, half-covered with ice, leaned in a silver bucket nearby. The omelet, higher and fluffier than any Juli had ever made, rested in a nest of parsley. There was a green salad and variety of dressing, plus a small tray of toast triangles. It was basically the same simple meal Juli had planned, yet far more impressively elegant.

Thorne seated her expertly, then just as expertly uncorked the bottle and poured some of the pale, bubbling liquid into Juli's glass.

"Champagne?" she gasped, disbelievingly.

"Of course. Aren't we celebrating a truce? A cessation of hostilities?"

Was he somehow making fun of her, Juli wondered uneasily, talking about a "truce"? But when he lifted his gracefully curved champagne glass, his tilted head and expression seemed merely questioning about her delay in responding to his gesture.

Juli lifted her glass. "A . . . a truce," she agreed tremulously. She sipped the champagne, her feelings a strange mixture of giddiness and pleasure and apprehension. The omelet was delicious, succulent with buttery bits of mushroom and delicately flavored shrimp. The Roquefort dressing for the salad was creamy-rich, the salad greens crisp. Juli let herself luxuriate in the richness of it all, refusing to let herself be upset by the unwanted thought that Thorne's cook, Estelle, was evidently not unaccustomed to whipping up elegant little late dinners for two.

Now Thorne seemed to have undergone yet another transformation. His conversation jumped lightly from subject to subject. He was full of amusing little anecdotes about the town and company and current events. Juli responded in a similarly light vein, exchanging a bit of amusing repartee with him about women's rights, keeping away from the emotionally and sexually charged atmosphere of the pool.

And yet in spite of the light, brisk conversation, Juli was aware of a rising tension between them. It was not the tension of anger that so often vibrated between them, however. It was more a tension of anticipation, as if an unknown force were carrying them higher and higher toward some breathless climax.

Estelle brought dessert and then discreetly retired. It was yet another almost sinfully rich concoction of angel-food cake and fresh strawberries and thick cream. Juli ate hers slowly, partly to savor the lush flavors, partly to postpone the climax toward which the evening seemed inevitably rising. And yet she hardly knew if she put it off because of reluctance or sweet anticipation. . . .

They finished the dessert and had another glass of champagne. How many had she had? Juli wondered a bit giddily. "I really must be going now," she said finally.

He eyed her lazily. "Surely you don't intend to eat and run. I thought you might stay . . . longer."

Juli felt a small tingle of alarm at that expressive pause between words. His eyes looked lazily heavy-lidded, but behind the relaxed expression she caught a gleam of something else. He didn't really think she was going to stay here all night, did he? She was in love with him. She knew he found her attractive and desirable. She also knew those feelings didn't necessarily balance out, that if something happened between them it would involve her heart, but perhaps only his body. But even if he didn't love her, she was uneasily aware of his expert ability to manipulate her through the treacherous demands of her own body, and in the end it was her heart that could come out the loser.

Smoothly, as if sensing her doubt and withdrawal, he changed the subject. "Before you go, would you like to see the pictures I took of the sunset the evening you climbed up to the ridge?"

"Oh, yes, I'd love to," Juli agreed eagerly,

relieved. Photography seemed a safe enough subject.

He led her to another room, a combination home office and den. Along the way he pointed out his darkroom.

"Brian was telling me that you're quite well known for your desert photography," Juli commented.

Thorne paused and eyed her reflectively for a moment before ushering her into the den. "Oh, yes, Brian Eames. Have you been seeing much of him?" He sounded disapproving before he even heard her answer.

"Not really," she said uncomfortably, wishing she hadn't mentioned Brian's name. "He did stop by the trailer one evening for a while."

Thorne made no comment. The wall switch turned on two lamps, revealing a pleasantly masculine room with a heavy walnut desk and bookshelves, several bronze sculptures of Western art, and a colorful Navajo Indian rug on the floor. The walls were decorated with desert scenes of mountains and cactuses and weathered buildings. A huge sectional sofa upholstered in lush chocolate-colored velvet filled one corner. Within the alcove formed by the corner sections of the sofa, an enormous burl of polished redwood served as a coffee table.

"Make yourself comfortable." He motioned with a careless wave toward the sofa. "Would you like coffee or something else to drink?"

"No, thank you." Hands held behind her, Juli wandered around the room, realizing that the pictures which she had at first thought were paintings were actually color photographs, so artistically done that they were art. No wonder, she thought, that he had handed back her sad little attempts at desert photography without comment.

Now he brought out a sheaf of color photographs, but before showing them to her he casually flicked a switch on a built-in stereo, and the sound of soft Spanish guitars drifted through the room. He set the photographs on the coffee table and sat down beside her on the soft luxury of the sofa.

The first few photographs were everything Juli had wanted to capture on film but hadn't when she climbed the ridge that other evening. She exclaimed over them, then went on to the next and in surprise saw a human figure among the saguaros in the distance, too far away to be recognizable, except that Juli knew who it was.

"Oh, look!" she said, laughing. "You caught me in one of your photographs."

"So I did," he agreed noncommittally.

In the next photograph she was close enough to be recognizable. Recognizable, too, was a certain determination written on her face as she crawled over a broken slab of boulder blocking her way. But the next photograph was the real shocker.

There was nothing of the sunset in it, just Juli. She was resting with one foot propped up on a rock, her body half-turned away from the camera as she looked at something in the distance, one hand caught in the gesture of brushing a strand of hair out of her eyes. Juli's lips parted and she felt color flood her face. She had no memory of the moment, and yet she looked posed with deliberate provocativeness, thrusting breasts sharply silhouetted, the halter top drooping on one side by the raised position of her arm to expose the inner curve of her breast. There was an embarrassingly impudent thrust to her hips, and even her facial expression, which must have had something to do with the sunset she was watching, looked dreamily sensual.

"Why, you must have been standing only

a few feet away from me!" Juli gasped. "But I don't remember that at all."

"Telephoto lens," Thorne said laconically.

"You mean you were deliberately taking photographs of me that I knew nothing about?" she asked, uncertain whether to be angry or flattered, and feeling a little of both. "That's almost like spying!"

"You were trespassing," he pointed out. "The photographs could have proved that, if it were ever necessary."

"Oh, come now," Juli scoffed. "You surely didn't think I was climbing up there to sabotage your house!"

"You were rather angry at me, as I recall," he reminded, but the devilish gleam in his eyes told her he was only teasing her now.

"Yes. Well, I've apologized," she said a little awkwardly. "And I really must be going now. I do want to thank you for a lovely day."

She started to rise, but the pressure of his hand on her arm detained her. It was not a harsh pressure, but neither could it be ignored.

"Listen to the music," he said softly.

Reluctantly, and yet held by some force that was stronger than her conscious will, she obeyed. The stereophonic sound from unseen speakers drifted through the room as if borne on a tropical breeze, as real as if softly strumming guitars were all around them. The music was delicate, now sad, now lilting, but always just beneath the surface was something else, a subtly sensual beat to which her pulse began to throb in response. He leaned back, one arm around her shoulders, gently pulling her head against his own shoulder.

She knew she should pull away, should jump and run, but those sensible messages from her mind had no power over her languid muscles, drugged by the warmth of his body, champagne, and the music. She seemed filled with a floating lassitude that made any conscious movement of her own impossible, not even when she felt Thorne shift their bodies so they were more lying than sitting on the lush sofa. His lips roamed her face, brushing her temples and eyelids, exploring the soft curve of her cheek and the pulsebeat in her throat. Her eyes were half-closed, his face a shadowy blur over her with a strand of dark hair falling across his forehead. The weight of his body, half over hers, was not unpleasant, and when his mouth found hers, her arms moved of their own volition to encircle his neck.

The kiss was gentle at first, but deepened as his mouth boldly explored hers. Tentatively at first, but with an increasing boldness of her own, her mouth explored, too.

There was no conversation. Words were superfluous, unnecessary to the way their mouths and bodies seemed meant for each other. He unfastened the top buttons of her blouse and slid the material aside to expose her shoulder, creamy-gold in the lamplight. The teasing touch of his tongue left a trail of fire across her shoulder and then dipped with practiced expertise to the curve of her breast, undaunted by the flimsy barrier of her lacy bra.

Juli's floating mind gave no heed to where all this was leading. She was simply floating down a corridor of exquisite pleasure where her senses were drowned in lush sound and sensuous caresses. The whisper of his lips in her ear didn't form words. She was only conscious of the husky sound of his voice, the feel of his warm breath on her ear. Then a certain urgency in his voice broke through.

"Let's go somewhere more comfortable — my room . . ." His lips teased the lobe of her ear.

"Your room?" she repeated, faint alarm

seeping into the dreamy, anesthetized swirls of her mind.

"I want you with me all night," he whispered huskily. "I want to wake up in the morning and find you there in my arms."

Her mind played with the tantalizing thought, and the love she felt for him surged through her in a hot flood. Yes . . . yes! She wanted to lie in his arms and wake up beside him! But not just for a night — for always.

That thought hit her like a sudden drench of cold water thrown in her face. She struggled to sit up, aware of her unbuttoned blouse and disheveled hair, her sandals fallen to the floor. His shirt was unbuttoned, too, and the lamplight glinted on his bronzed chest and the dark hair slanting across his forehead.

"What's the matter?" he demanded, raising up on one elbow beside her.

What was the matter? she thought dizzily. She wanted love and he offered sex. She wanted a lifetime and he offered a night. She wanted his heart — but all that could come of this was her own heartbreak. And yet another part of her fiercely demanded that she throw cautious reason to the wind and take the temporary ecstasy he offered, however brief it might be. Recklessly, she was ready to give in to that demand when another shocking thought stabbed her. Had Thorne deliberately *not* fixed the water this evening in order to maneuver her into this very position? Had he deliberately calculated and cold-bloodedly planned to seduce her for a night's pleasure and then go back to the arms of his true love, Nicole?

"What's the matter?" he repeated, more roughly this time.

"I don't know. . . ." Her voice was tremulous. "I'm not sure. I feel so confused. . . ."

"Confused? About what?" he demanded. "You want me as much as I want you. I know you do."

It was true. Her body almost ached with wanting him. But the trouble was, she wanted so much more than he did.

"I don't get this," he said, his voice tight with anger now. "You lead me on until I'm half-crazy with wanting you, and then you go all coy and tearful —"

"I led *you* on!" Juli gasped. "After you . . . you practically attacked me in the pool and fed me champagne and —"

"Oh, come on now," he scoffed harshly. "I haven't done a single thing you weren't already willing and eager to do. And don't tell me staying the night wasn't a part of your clever little scheme."

He sat up and started buttoning his shirt. One of the buttons tangled in the material and he yanked at it so savagely the material ripped and the button flew across the room. Juli was still almost in shock, still trying to understand his angry words, and her own feelings were as yet unformed into anger.

"What do you mean by that?" she gasped in bewilderment.

"That phony business about the water," he said contemptuously. "Do you think I'm so damned stupid I couldn't figure out that you'd flipped off the switch to the pump at the electrical box? Oh, yes, you had it all figured out before we ever left the trailer this morning. I thought you were so sweet and innocent, unlike most of the women I know, but instead you're just another cheap, conniving little schemer. And then when I respond just the way you plan, you suddenly get cold feet and go all coy and scared. You might at least be woman enough to go through with it!"

Juli felt totally bewildered, shriveled by the hot blast of his angry tirade. His face was dark with fury, the gray-green eyes brilliantly dangerous. She had the panicky feeling that in this frame of mind he was capable of doing anything. She was aware that they were alone and she was helpless against his superior strength and fury. What had happened to that warm, companionable nature she had found in him today? Was that human, accessible side of him only a pretense that disappeared whenever he met opposition? Or perhaps it was even less than that, she thought unhappily. Perhaps it had never even existed outside her own naïve, hopeful imagination.

But she still couldn't really comprehend what he was accusing her of. "You think I tried . . . I deliberately planned to seduce you? That I deliberately did something to the pump so you would have to invite me over here?" She shook her head at the incredulousness of this idea. "Even *if* I wanted to arrange such a thing, I wouldn't have the slightest idea how to —"

Juli broke off suddenly, her mouth forming an O of surprised remembrance. Though not with the deliberate intent he suggested, she evidently *had* turned the pump off. Last night when she was at the electrical box with the flashlight, she had flipped several switches back and forth, trying to make the lights come back on. She must have turned off the switch to the pump and then, when the lights blinked on, not switched it back to the proper position.

But to have Thorne think she had done such a thing with the deliberate intent of seducing him and spending the night with him — ! Of all the colossal, egotistical, incredible nerve! Juli's shock and incredulousness suddenly lumped into cold fury. She stood up and furiously stuffed the tail of her blouse into the waist of her pants.

"What are you doing?" he asked, eyes narrowed.

"I think it's obvious that I'm dressing," she snapped. She fumbled the buttons of her blouse through the buttonholes.

His hand shot out and caught the silky material at her throat, both of them aware that with one jerk he could rip the blouse open to her waist. "Little girls who tease sometimes find they have to pay off," he said with dangerous softness.

She held her back rigid. "I'm going home now," she stated defiantly.

"Oh, no, you're not." His voice was grim. "You schemed and planned to spend the night in my bed. And that is exactly what you're going to do."

Chapter Eight

Thorne locked his powerful grip around her arm and shoved her roughly down the hallway. He hardly looked at her, yanking her along like some animal on the end of a leash when she balked.

"You can't do this!" Juli stormed, furious at him and angry with herself, too, because the protest came out squeaky instead of commanding.

He paused beside a closed door. "Can't I?" he taunted.

Juli tried to pull away, but there was no escaping the iron grip on her arm, cruel and impersonal as a shackle. "I . . . I'll scream!"

He lifted an eyebrow and waited for her to make good on the threat. Juli swallowed convulsively, knowing that even if she tried to scream, little sound would come from her dry throat. And what good would it do? Would Estelle come running to the rescue? Hardly. Her blouse had come unbuttoned again and she clutched at it with her free hand.

With another contemptuous glance at her, Thorne shoved the door open and flipped a light switch that turned on a lamp by the bed. Even in her state of shock, Juli was aware of a rugged elegance about the room that reflected Thorne's personality. The bedroom was thoroughly masculine, yet at the same time luxurious, with a king-sized bed covered with a spread in a bold Aztec design, paneled walls, corner fireplace, lush gold-brown carpeting, and mirrored closets. She caught a glimpse of her own disheveled reflection, eyes wide and dark, skin pale. Next to Thorne's tall, powerful figure, she looked almost fragile and helplessly at his mercy. She dragged her feet as he yanked her toward the enormous bed, and with a growl of impatience he swept her up in his arms and threw her across the bed.

She lay there for a moment, frozen with panic, then scrambled to the far side of the bed. She grabbed the only weapon she could reach, a downy pillow, realizing how foolish and flimsy a defense it was, and yet facing him defiantly with it.

Thorne stood there looking down at her, hands clenching and unclenching, as if he fought with something within himself. His chiseled lips had a twist of contempt, but desire still gleamed in his eyes, dark as a stormy green sea.

Juli huddled on the bed, not knowing if she was more afraid of his contempt or his desire. In this mood he seemed capable of anything, an untamed savage driven more by angry desire than reason. She didn't try to escape from the bed. He was between her and the door. Slowly she pulled herself up on the bed, her eyes never leaving his, until her back was against the headboard.

He took a menacing step toward her. "I ought to —" he growled. He broke off, lips compressed. Then his voice went hard and flat. "I turned on the switch to the pump at the trailer. I think you'll find your water problems solved when you return."

With that he spun on his heel and slammed the door as he stalked out. Juli lay there a moment, too astonished to move, then leaped to her feet and darted to the door. With trembling fingers she turned the lock on the knob, though that hardly seemed necessary with the sound of his angry footsteps thudding down the hallway.

Juli leaned weakly against the door. Had he changed his mind at the last minute about forcing her to submit to his will? Or had it all been a bluff? Whatever the reason, relief flooded over her as she massaged her arm, numbed by his tight grip.

But as the feeling came back into Juli's arm, angry outrage replaced that first instinctive surge of relief. How dare he throw her in this room like some sort of harem prisoner? This was twentieth-century Arizona, not some medieval kingdom in which women were treated like chattel! Well, he needn't think he was going to get away with this, she thought furiously, because she was not about to spend the night in this bedroom, no matter how luxurious it might be. She would simply —

Her thoughts broke off and she slowly dropped to the edge of the huge bed. She would simply *what?* Walk home across the ridge in the dark? She would be a pincushion before she got halfway to the trailer.

She would simply call a cab! That seemed a reasonable solution, and her glance darted around the room searching for a phone. There was none. Thorne, she thought wryly, was obviously not the type of man who wanted to be interrupted in bed by the ringing of a phone. So she would find a phone somewhere else. She had her hand on the doorknob before she paused with second thoughts. There were undoubtedly phones at various locations in the house, but she would first have to find one. What if she ran into Thorne again? That thought sent a shiver up her spine. He had, for now at least, evidently decided to leave her alone, but if she roused his anger further . . .

And then another dismaying thought struck her. Thorne's thorough mind had undoubtedly already considered the thought that she might call a cab, and by now he had surely closed the exterior gates to the estate so a cab couldn't even get to the house.

So it appeared, she decided reluctantly, that she was stuck here for the night. She took another, longer look around the room, grudgingly admiring the earthy colors and lush materials. She walked over to glance into the bathroom. Sage-green towels hung neatly on the racks, and the dressing table held an assortment of masculine toiletry items. Boldly, she inspected the closets, too, half-expecting to find one full of Nicole's clothes, but there were only Thorne's well-cut business suits and other more casual attire.

Then she stood in the center of the dimly lit room wondering what to do next. She debated about going back to the den

197

for her purse, but decided against it because of the risk of encountering Thorne again. She would pick it up in the morning, along with her bathing suit and other clothes out in the bathhouse. On reflection, however, she was not sure she ever wanted to see that bathing suit again, much less wear it, because she knew it would always remind her of this humiliating evening.

She took a brief, stinging shower and slid naked between sheets that felt cool and silky to her bare skin. She was determined that at first break of dawn, as soon as there was light enough to make her way safely across the ridge, she would be up and gone.

But sleep would not come. Partly it was because she was still suspicious of Thorne's intentions, doubtful that even a locked door would keep him out if he made up his mind he wanted back into the bedroom. Partly it was because of the unfamiliar feel of the silky sheets against her naked skin. Back home, on hot nights, she occasionally slept without a nightgown, but here the lack made her feel uncomfortably vulnerable. The contemptuous curl of Thorne's lips said he had no desire to touch her, but the look in his eyes had contradicted that. Would he change his mind and return?

She propped herself up in bed with the pillows and kept a wary eye aimed in the direction of the door to the hall. Where was Thorne now? What was he doing? Her mind went back over his incredible accusation. He really believed she had deliberately tampered with the pump and schemed to spend the night here with him. She remembered her feeble attempt to deter him from going out to the pump house. That probably helped prove to him his suspicions were correct! And he also thought she had deliberately led him on here at the house and then backed out at the last minute. Of all the colossal, insufferable, egotistical nerve! Did he consider himself so irresistibly attractive that every woman he met was out to seduce and ensnare him?

And yet, with a small twinge of guilt, she remembered that she had also wondered if he had deliberately *not* fixed the pump so she would have to accept his invitation to come here. Was thinking that also colossal ego on her part? Oh, she felt so mixed up and confused!

It was all so unfair! *He* was the one who had teased and tantalized and challenged her all evening. What woman wouldn't respond to the romantic setting and the champagne and his expert lovemaking? Why should he then be contemptuous because she did respond? Perhaps his real fury came because things hadn't worked out the way *he* had planned, because she hadn't fallen all the way into his seductive trap.

And how dare he act so self-righteous? she thought with fresh anger. Now she recognized the struggle that had gone on within him at various times during the evening. He had been struggling with the temptation to be unfaithful to Nicole — a battle, she thought scornfully, that he had lost. If it hadn't been for Juli herself finally coming to her senses before —

Her thoughts broke off abruptly. She didn't want to think about what might have happened, and one part of her recognized guiltily that this was because she was at least halfway regretful that it hadn't happened.

Of course, she thought slowly, she could have told him how the pump really came to be turned off. A stiffening of her pride rejected that thought immediately. He had already decided she was some scheming little tramp, and she was not about to beg him humbly to change his mind. He probably wouldn't believe her, anyway. There was another reason for not explaining, too, she realized reluctantly. She was afraid she would break down and reveal she loved him, and she couldn't do that, not ever, after he had made plain what he really thought of her.

The unhappy fact was that no matter what had happened, she was in love with him, she thought despairingly. And that was where her anger got all mixed up with hurt and pain and shame. He had humiliated and degraded her with his cynical, scathing accusation — but she loved him, anyway.

She was exhausted both from the long hike and the emotional collision with Thorne, but she stayed awake for what seemed like hours, tossing and turning in the huge bed while thoughts and images chased back and forth through her mind. She was determined to be out of the house before Thorne even woke up in the morning, and that resolution further contributed to her restless night.

But when she finally awoke from a dead, dreamless sleep in the morning, she was instantly aware that her plans had already gone awry. Her watch was in her purse, but she could tell from the sunlight peeking through the drapes that the hour was not early. She hastily washed her face and dressed and then tiptoed cautiously down the hall toward the den. She jumped as a figure met her in the doorway.

"Oh, Miss Townsend, you're up!" Estelle exclaimed. "I'll have your breakfast ready in just a few minutes. Would you like to eat in the dining room, or out on the patio?"

Juli was about to decline breakfast and murmur that she was just leaving, but instead something prompted her to ask tentatively, "Has Thorne — Mr. Taylor — had breakfast yet?"

"Oh, my, yes. He left for the office over an hour ago. He took the pickup and said you were to use the Porsche when you . . . um . . . needed transportation."

Estelle was obviously practiced at being tactful, Juli thought with wry amusement. She was about to decline that offer, also, and hurry away with all possible speed, but a sudden reckless defiance stopped her. There was no need to rush now. Thorne was gone for the day. Why not enjoy her moment of luxury? "Breakfast on the patio would be lovely," she said firmly.

Juli went on into the den, no longer tiptoeing, and found her purse and sandals. She ignored the pictures on the coffee table. The sofa pillows had already been neatly straightened by the efficient Estelle. On the way back to Thorne's bedroom, Juli boldly peered into open doors. Thorne, she thought defiantly, probably expected some such uncouth behavior from a girl of her type, anyway. She saw two guest bedrooms, one with a warm peach-color scheme, the other a sunny lemon-yellow. Thorne, she realized with a small jolt, had evidently slept in the lilac-colored bedroom right next to his own bedroom, where she was sleeping. The bed covers were mussed and rumpled, as if he had slept restlessly, also. With another jolt she saw a door opening off the side of the bedroom. It couldn't be — but it was! When she yanked it open she was looking directly at Thorne's king-sized bed, still rumpled from her own restless tossings and turnings. How Thorne must have laughed at her, she thought furiously, knowing all the time there was an unlocked door between them.

Outside on the patio she tried to calm her thoughts. Nothing had happened. Thorne was gone now. She could relax.

She settled herself in a cushioned red-wood lounge chair on the patio. The sunshine felt deliciously warm, and Estelle arrived a few minutes later with breakfast on a tray that fit neatly across the arms of the chair. There was freshly squeezed orange juice, crisp bacon, soft-boiled eggs, and an airy pastry that literally melted in her mouth. With a sigh of pure pleasure, Juli leaned back to enjoy a second cup of coffee from the little pot on the tray. Deliberately, she put all thoughts of last night's unpleasantness out of her mind and played a little lady-of-the-manor fantasy game. She imagined herself sitting here each morning, planning a busy day, then entertaining around the pool in the evening. From there it wasn't hard to imagine greeting a returning husband at the patio gate with a kiss, and there would be a couple of children tumbling happily around her feet. . . .

She laughed at herself and her wild imaginings, but it was a certain bittersweetness about the images that made her quickly turn her mind elsewhere. It was time she was going. She stood up and stretched cat-like in the sun, reluctant to walk away and leave all this for the stuffiness of the trailer. Perhaps just a short swim before she departed, she decided. Thorne would never know.

She found her bathing suit where she

had left it in the bathhouse. A moment later she slipped into the silky warmth of the pool. She sidestroked and swam underwater, floated dreamily on her back and found fairy castles and furry animals in the cloud patterns in the sky. She was just watching a billow of cloud form itself into a benevolent moon face when she was startled by the sound of a car door slamming in the driveway. She floundered in the water, grabbing for the side. Was Thorne returning already? No, he couldn't be!

Then she heard laughter and female voices. Who could it be? Whoever it was, she surely did not want to be found here and have to meet curious eyes and perhaps make awkward explanations about her presence. She would just dash into the bathhouse, change her clothes, and slip out the back way before anyone saw her.

She swung lithely out of the pool and started toward the bathhouse, but too late she realized the women were not approaching the front door of the house. They were coming through the patio gate! Halfway to the bathhouse, dripping puddles of water and feeling nakedly exposed in the burgundy bathing suit, Juli met them.

One was Nicole, dressed in a plain white

dress dramatized with a heavy silver and turquoise Indian squash-blossom necklace and silver concho belt. Her mouth literally dropped open when she saw Juli. The other woman was older, but slim and petite and feminine, with perfectly groomed white hair and pink linen pantsuit.

Nicole quickly recovered her composure. "Miss Townser, I believe it is?" she said, voice chilly enough to goosebump Juli's skin.

"Townsend. Juli Townsend," Juli corrected weakly, knowing full well Nicole had deliberately mispronounced her name to put her in her place. With a sinking sensation, Juli also knew that the older woman, in spite of a lack of physical resemblance, must be Thorne's mother.

That suspicion was confirmed when the older woman graciously introduced herself after Nicole failed to make any introductions.

"I'm so pleased to meet you," Juli murmured automatically. It was hardly true, of course, at least not under these circumstances. Juli felt as if she were blushing from head to toe. Her breakfast tray was still on the lounge chair. It was plain as a billboard announcement that she had spent the night here. Awkwardly, she explained about her water problems at the trailer and Thorne's hospitality, but from the frozen smile on Nicole's face and the slightly amused expression on Mrs. Taylor's, Juli knew her explanation was only making things worse. It hardly sounded believable even to her own ears. Nicole finally interrupted impatiently.

"Is Thorne here now? I see his car outside."

"No, he went to the office sometime ago. I believe he drove his pickup."

"I'll call and tell him we've arrived," Mrs. Taylor said. She started toward the door, adding over her shoulder, "He wasn't expecting us this early."

Nicole's eyes moved disdainfully over Juli's body. "Obviously," she said scathingly, loud enough only for Juli to hear.

Juli scooted off to dress, angrily berating herself for not having gotten out the minute she woke up. Why, oh, *why,* had she hung around playing her foolish little fantasy game with luxury? She took all the time she possibly could dressing and applying a touch of lip gloss and eyeshadow, not wanting to be alone with Nicole. With relief she heard Mrs. Taylor return and say to Nicole that Thorne would be out to join them for lunch.

Juli took a deep breath and stepped out into the brilliant sunshine, her exit dialogue all planned. "It's been lovely meeting you, Mrs. Taylor," she said brightly, head held high, "and so nice seeing you again, Nicole. I must be going now, to take care of my water problems, so if you'll excuse me — ?"

"Oh, but you mustn't leave now," Mrs. Taylor protested firmly. "Thorne was very definite about your staying for lunch, and I'm sure you know how disagreeable he can be if his wishes are ignored." She smiled at Juli in a conspiratorial way, as if knowledge of Thorne's arrogance made a bond between them.

Juli was totally astonished, but no more so than Nicole, she realized, glancing at the young woman.

Nicole's usual glossy composure was shattered for the second time that morning. "But . . . but if Juli has to leave —" she faltered. "I mean, she said something about water problems. . . ." Nicole looked thoroughly discomfited, and one carefully manicured hand toyed nervously with the handsome necklace. Gathering herself together, however, she managed to bring some of the aloof chill back into her voice. "We certainly would not want to cause

Miss Townsend any inconvenience."

Juli hesitated uncertainly. She did not want to stay and suffer through an uncomfortable luncheon, and a certain stubbornness within her rebelled at complying with Thorne's arrogant orders after the way he had treated her last night. But neither did she like the idea of meekly giving in to Nicole's anxious determination to get rid of her. And she had to admit to a certain curiosity. Why did Thorne want her to stay?

Mrs. Taylor, however, seemed to consider the matter already settled. Obviously, from her point of view, what Thorne wanted, Thorne got. She took off her pink jacket and stretched out in a lounge chair. "My, it feels so good to be home."

With a meaningful glance at Juli, Nicole agreed. "Yes, it does feel good." She was obviously making the point that this was, or soon would be, her home, also.

It was not, Juli thought grimly, going to be a pleasant morning or luncheon. She decided to abandon her stubbornness. She was not going to stay and suffer Nicole's taunts or the possibility of some further humiliation from Thorne. But Mrs. Taylor's next words stopped her.

"I called from the telephone in the den,

and I couldn't help but notice the photographs on the coffee table," she remarked. "I was surprised because Thorne so seldom photographs people. He has kind of a 'thing' about it, in fact, and has been known to walk miles to avoid having people in a particular shot he wants."

Juli murmured something noncommittal, glad that now only her face could reveal the blush that seemed to cover her whole body again. Had Mrs. Taylor looked at *all* the photographs, especially that suggestive closeup?

"Thorne took photographs of Miss Townsend?" Nicole snapped in surprise.

"It was probably just an accident," Juli said weakly, but they all knew Thorne was too much of a perfectionist to make any such slip.

Not more than sixty seconds later Nicole excused herself, saying she wanted to get some things from the car. She made no pretense of heading for the car, however, and Juli knew she was rushing directly to the den to examine those photographs.

Mrs. Taylor's gaze followed Nicole thoughtfully for a moment, then she turned back to Juli. "Are you a visitor or a permanent resident here in Cholla?" she asked pleasantly.

Cautiously at first, but with growing ease as she realized Mrs. Taylor was sincerely interested, Juli explained about David's death and Aunt Kate and the trailer, finally going on to mention even David's almost fanatical obsession with the lost gold mine. The only thing she left out was David's accusation that Mrs. Taylor's other son, Jason, had somehow cheated David in the past. Juli had found nothing to substantiate that accusation, and now she wondered if perhaps it were not just some dark, suspicious quirk in David's mind, some mistaken perception of reality. He had also, she remembered, intimated to his mother that he was head of the research department at Taylor Electronics, which was certainly not true.

Mrs. Taylor nodded sympathetically now and then. She was a good listener and Juli was a little embarrassed when she realized how long she had been babbling on. Somehow it seemed more important than ever to make clear to Mrs. Taylor that Juli had not spent the night *with* Thorne. "I'd like you to know I stayed here last night because I really didn't have any water at the trailer," she said hurriedly. "At least I thought I didn't," she added, realizing helplessly that her explanations only seemed to get more complicated.

Mrs. Taylor smiled. "I'm glad my son was properly hospitable," she said non-committally. Nicole returned just as Mrs. Taylor added, "I don't suppose you'll be staying in Cholla much longer?"

"It all depends on how long it takes to sell David's trailer and property," Juli said.

She was aware of an odd look on Nicole's face, as if Nicole were re-appraising her after seeing her through the eyes of Thorne's camera, suspecting Thorne had some special interest in her. There was a certain amount of grim satisfaction for Juli in Nicole's sudden recognition of Juli as real competition. That satisfaction was short-lived, however, wilting under Juli's inescapable memories of last night. Nicole, in the end, would be the real winner. The photographs meant nothing.

The morning passed with surprising ease and quickness. Nicole was almost silent, her expression sullen and wary. She obviously disbelieved Juli's explanation of her presence here. Mrs. Taylor carried most of the conversation with anecdotes about her stay in Acapulco. She stayed away from the subject of Thorne, evidently feeling a more neutral subject was safer.

Shortly after twelve o'clock, Thorne arrived. He came through the patio gate, well

212

dressed in a slate-blue suit and a pale blue shirt. With the practiced ease of a man assessing a situation quickly, his gaze flicked across the faces of the three women waiting for him. At least two of those women were tense and nervous. Thorne, however, appeared not at all uncomfortable with the situation. He kissed his mother warmly, nodded pleasantly first to Nicole, then to Juli. He pulled up a chair and sat between Juli and Nicole.

Juli watched him warily out of the corner of her eye while he small-talked with his mother about her flight up from Acapulco, waiting for him to explain about Juli's presence. Surely he must be as eager as she was to make plain to his mother and Nicole that he and Juli had not spent the night together, no matter how the situation might appear on the surface.

Thorne, however, seemed in no hurry to make explanations. He chatted affably about the company's picnic and barbecue, mentioned that the new construction plans were right on schedule, and made chatty comments about the hike into the Superstitions.

After a while Juli angrily suspected that he was deliberately postponing the explanation, enjoying seeing her squirm with embarrassment. Finally, meaning to bring this uncomfortable little game to an end, she determinedly broached the subject herself. "I was telling your mother and Nicole earlier that I stayed here last night because —"

"I hope I didn't disturb you when I got up this morning," he interrupted, his voice unexpectedly intimate as he turned to look at her with wide, innocent eyes. "I'm afraid I was rather noisy getting my clothes out of the closet."

Juli looked at him aghast as realization of the meaning of his words dawned on her. He had used that adjoining door this morning, had seen her sleeping in his bed. *Sleeping naked* . . . She swallowed convulsively.

"I didn't wake you when I got up because I thought you needed the rest after —" He paused, smiling suggestively, and only Nicole's startled gasp interrupted the pregnant silence. "After our long hike yesterday," he finally finished.

Smoothly, he immediately turned back to his mother and went on talking about some mutual friends, giving Juli no time to vent the outrage she felt. He had told no untruths, yet he had left the completely false impression that he and Juli had spent the night together in the same bed. And that suggestive pause had implied her exhaustion was from something far more intimate than a hike together!

And he had done it all *deliberately.* Why? To amuse himself and humiliate her? If so, he had certainly succeeded. She felt as if a permanent blazing blush had settled on her face.

What, she wondered in an agony of embarrassment, was Mrs. Taylor thinking now? The expression on Mrs. Taylor's calm face was perfectly neutral, relaxed, and pleasant as she chatted with Thorne. Only the occasional quick, speculative dart of her eyes between Juli and Nicole betrayed any hint that her mind was on anything other than the inconsequential conversation. By now she must surely think that Juli had lied to her about last night, or at least not told the complete truth.

Juli was tempted to bring the conversation to a screeching halt by bluntly demanding that Thorne make plain that he and Juli had *not* spent the night together. What stopped her was a certain apprehension that Thorne would somehow twist her demand to suit his own purposes and somehow cleverly manage to humiliate her further. Better to maintain an embarrassed silence and keep reminding herself that after today she would probably never see any of these people again. Silently, she cursed Thorne for inflicting this humiliation on her, cursed herself with even greater vehemence for allowing herself to be drawn into this ridiculous situation.

The only satisfaction Juli had was a realization that sooner or later Thorne was going to pay dearly for whatever enjoyment he was getting out of this little game, because he was obviously making Nicole furious. She sat there with her hands clenched so tightly that her perfectly manicured nails bit into her soft palms.

Thorne seemed oblivious to Nicole's anger, smiling and chatting easily. Estelle served lunch on a round redwood table in a shady area of the patio. Thorne gallantly seated his mother, his hand dropping lightly to touch Juli's shoulder as he passed her to take his own seat. Nicole watched with a venomous stare that included both Thorne and Juli in her fury.

Juli determinedly tried to concentrate on the food, a delicious salad with huge pink prawns ringing a bowl of spicy sauce in the center of the dish. With the salad were warm, soft tortillas, buttered and rolled into slim tubes for easy eating, and icy lemonade. Concentration was not easy, however, with Thorne sitting right next to her. He carried the conversation during the meal, but he made no effort to correct his earlier insinuations that Juli and he had slept together. In fact, he made several more minor remarks that only served to emphasize the misconception. Once he remarked that he hoped she had found the king-sized bed large enough to be comfortable last night, and another time he commented teasingly on her reaction to champagne. Several times he actually touched her, not intimately, but with the familiar ease of lovers, and Juli was as baffled by her own reactions to the touches as she was by Thorne's strange behavior. She was furious with the way he was embarrassing and humiliating her, deliberately making her look like some cheap young thing with whom he had amused himself for a night. And yet in spite of that, each grazing touch sent a warm, alive tingle through her body that she desperately tried to ignore. A certain gleam in Thorne's eyes told her he was not unaware of his effect on her in spite of her effort to appear nonchalant.

If it were not that she felt so uncomfortable herself, Juli thought ruefully, she might have found a certain perverse pleasure in Nicole's angry squirmings. Nicole picked at her food, turned and twitched in her chair as if the cushion were made of cactus. She stabbed murderous glances at both Juli and Thorne, and what little she had to say she delivered in a voice dripping with acid.

Juli was completely baffled. Didn't Thorne realize Nicole was ready to scratch his eyes out? Was he willing to risk Nicole's anger simply to humiliate and embarrass Juli?

Then, with another totally unexpected remark from Thorne, Juli's perspective suddenly changed and she caught her breath in surprise.

Addressing his mother, Thorne said casually, "Juli and I were talking about driving down to Tucson someday soon. I thought she might like to see the San Xavier del Bac mission." He turned to Juli. "Are you still interested?"

Juli's lips parted. Yesterday they had discussed in the most casual of terms the possibility of driving down to Tucson and the mission sometime. After last night's fiasco, Juli had assumed their tenuous relationship was over, no matter what her secret feelings for him might be. Was this rather oblique invitation his way of saying he was sorry about last night, that he wanted to see her again? Was he oblivious to Nicole's anger because he really didn't care how she felt? Was his letting his mother and Nicole believe he and Juli had spent the night together not an attempt to humiliate and embarrass Juli, but a defiant announcement of his feelings for her? He was watching her now, waiting for her reaction, his eyes more wary than taunting.

"I . . . I'd really like to see the mission," Juli faltered. Then, recklessly, she rushed on. "This time I'll try not to do something so foolish as turn the pump off by accident." In a flurry of words, she explained how she had fumbled with the electrical switches when the power went off, accidentally leaving the pump switch turned off. She directed most of the explanation to Mrs. Taylor, but it was Thorne to whom she was really explaining, and she was certain he knew it.

Thorne listened without comment, his expression so inscrutable Juli couldn't tell whether or not he believed her. Nicole looked bored and impatient, Mrs. Taylor interested but noncommittal. An awkward silence ensued when Juli was finished.

Mrs. Taylor broke it by pleasantly changing the subject. "I saw the lovely photographs you took of Juli. I've never understood why you've always avoided photographing people when you do it so nicely."

"I thought you made it a *rule* not to photograph people," Nicole interjected sourly.

Thorne barely glanced at Nicole. Instead, with a meaningful look at Juli, he said, "There is an old saying that rules are made to be broken. I'm sure that is especially true with a subject as photogenic as Juli."

He smiled at her, a smile that unexpectedly rocketed her to dizzying heights. He *was* trying to make up and apologize for all that had happened last night, and he was doing it where it mattered most, where Nicole could not fail to see. All Juli's anger and suspicions melted in a blaze of feeling that she was suddenly afraid exposed her love for all the world to see She felt glad and tremulous and frightened and hopeful all rolled together. Whatever had gone wrong between them last night was nothing that couldn't be straightened out. Thorne's apology was hardly a humble pleading for forgiveness, but coming from him she knew it meant more than the most abject of apologies from many other men.

Finally, Thorne glanced at his watch and stood up. "Having lunch with three beautiful ladies has been most enjoyable, but it's time I was getting back to work. Juli, would you walk with me to the gate? There's something I'd like to discuss with you."

Juli set her glass on the table and wiped damp hands on a napkin. She felt as if she had been on an emotional roller coaster ride during the last twenty-four hours, swooping up or down as Thorne's whim directed. And now the ride was about to come to some kind of a conclusion.

Chapter Nine

They walked to the gate, Juli's heart thundering and her back feeling the stab of Nicole's venomous glances. It gave her an odd feeling to realize jealousy was behind Nicole's anger. Nicole, beautiful, pampered, and half-owner of the company, was jealous of *her.* That thought was forgotten as they reached the gate and she wondered frantically what Thorne was going to say. Did he want to talk to her about last night or the trip to Tucson? Perhaps admit he was wrong in his accusations? But she couldn't let him take all the blame for what had almost happened between them last night. She had wanted it, too. Thorne opened the gate, neither of them having yet spoken a word.

"What did you want to discuss?" Juli faltered.

Without answering, he took her hand and pulled her partway through the open gate. With a deft gesture he slid his other arm around her waist and molded her body against his.

A small gasp escaped Juli's startled lips. He hadn't pulled the gate shut. Mrs. Taylor's back was to them, but they were in Nicole's full view and Juli knew Thorne must be aware of that fact.

"Thorne — please, people are watching!" She made a small effort to pull back.

He grinned, a devil-may-care flash of white teeth, and only held her more tightly. "Let them watch."

"Thorne, really, maybe we should talk —"

"We've talked too much already. I can say everything there is to say like this."

With calm deliberateness, his other arm encircled her back and his dark head bent to meet her lips. And in that instant Juli forgot everything — forgot Nicole's spiteful gaze, forgot everything except the feel of his mouth and his hard, masculine body, forgot everything except the wild rapture of being in the arms of the man she loved.

Juli took a cab home a few minutes later. The Porsche was still out front for her use, but a remnant of pride that lingered beneath her joy kept her from using it. Because, if she took Thorne's car to the trailer, Thorne obviously would be obligated to come and get it. She wanted to do nothing that could possibly be construed as conniving or scheming on her part to manipulate Thorne into doing anything.

She was vaguely aware of the angry glitter in Nicole's eyes, but now she felt a sort of pity for the older girl. Juli knew it was jealousy that prompted the anger, and she had felt those searing pangs herself when she earlier thought Thorne was in love with Nicole. Even now she had to admit to a small twinge of her own jealousy in the knowledge that Nicole would be right there in the house with Thorne with every opportunity to work her charms on him. Charms to which Thorne had earlier not been immune . . .

Resolutely, she put such thoughts out of her mind. Nothing was going to mar her happiness this wonderful day, not with the feel of Thorne's mouth still burning on hers, not with the look in his eyes promising far more to come. Whatever had happened in the past was all over now, and Thorne had seemed not only immune to, but quite oblivious to, Nicole's charms today. Not that Nicole had been exactly charming, Juli thought with a certain wry amusement as she remembered Nicole's venomous glances and acid voice.

When the cab let her off at the trailer, Juli felt as if she had been gone days or weeks, rather than hours. The real estate salesman's card was stuck in the door, showing he had been there while she was gone. There was also a note from Brian. He sounded a bit querulous as he wrote that since she had no phone with which he could contact her that he had driven out Sunday evening and then found she wasn't home. He left a phone number and asked her to call him.

She intended to call him. She really did intend to, but the truth was she simply forgot all about him until his car pulled into the yard Tuesday evening. Her mind had been too full of thoughts of Thorne, full of the wonder of her love for him and the growing feeling that her love was returned.

"You're certainly a hard person to get hold of," he grumbled as he came up the trailer steps. "I was beginning to get worried about you."

"No need to worry. I've just been busy," Juli said brightly. She peered out the door at the clouds glowering over the ridge. "I think it's going to rain."

"It's about time," Brian snorted. "Day after day of sunshine just isn't *normal*. You never have a day just to lie around and feel grumpy and blame it all on the weather."

Juli laughed. "You seem to be managing."

Brian laughed, too. "I think I'm grumpy because I came out hoping to take you to a movie Sunday evening and you weren't here. I can see I'm going to have to take up sending smoke signals . . . or making plans further in advance."

Juli had the feeling he was about to issue some invitation she would probably hurt his feelings by rejecting, and she quickly interrupted with an offer of coffee.

He added cream and sugar after she poured coffee and set the cup in front of him. "I hoped I'd have something more helpful to report about your cousin David, but I'm afraid all I've learned is more of the same."

It seemed so long ago that Juli had found David's papers about the lost gold mine that it was with a sense of shock that she realized she had never told Brian about any of her findings. Very briefly she did so now, concluding, "It was unfair of me to be so suspicious of Taylor Electronics' offer to Aunt Kate. I know now that they're under no obligation, not even a moral one, to pay her anything. It was just a very generous gesture on Thorne's — Mr. Taylor's — part."

Brian glanced up sharply at her use of Thorne's first name, but he made no comment on it. "I think *you* are the one being generous, or naïve, if you think Thorne Taylor did anything out of pure generosity," he said cynically. "He and his lawyers and accountants probably figured it all out very carefully on a cost/benefit ratio. A sweet little old lady suing the company could make for very bad publicity."

Thorne had said practically the same thing himself, but somehow the statement grated on Juli's ears coming with Brian's measured cynicism. "I'm just glad Aunt Kate is getting the money," Juli said finally, half-annoyed because, the way Brian phrased it, she did come off sounding naïve for believing Thorne had been generous. But then, she thought firmly, Brian didn't know Thorne the way she did.

"Nicole Taylor was at the plant today," Brian went on unexpectedly. "I understand she gets the urge every once in a while to play company owner and throw her weight around. Probably another reason Thorne Taylor would like to get a ring on her finger as quick as he can. He'd no doubt have a little more control over her then."

Juli tried to conceal a quick stab of dismay. She put her cup down so the sudden tremor in her hand wouldn't be so obvious. "From what I've seen, Nicole is probably the one in a hurry," she suggested.

"Hard to tell," Brian reflected. "I'd say she holds all the high cards. Thorne needs her more than she needs him. He'd be in a real fix if she up and married someone else the way she married Jason so suddenly. Thorne would find half the company completely out from under his control, and I'm sure he's not about to let that happen."

"Do you think she's interested in someone else?" Juli asked tentatively.

"I imagine Thorne wonders what she does with her evenings up in Scottsdale," Brian said, nodding his head sagely. "He's not about to forget how she threw him over once to marry someone else and that she might do it again."

"She must wonder what he does with his evenings here in Cholla," Juli returned.

"True," Brian agreed. He laughed. "Somehow I have the feeling they deserve each other."

"But surely you don't think a man would marry purely for business reasons, do you?" Juli protested. "I mean, a man like Thorne Taylor seems too —" Juli broke off awkwardly. The word that came to her mind to describe Thorne was *passionate,* and she didn't dare use that. "Surely a man like Thorne Taylor would think love was important, too."

Brian reached across the plastic-topped table and patted her hand as if she were a child. "Juli, you are naïve. You don't think

Thorne is going to let a little thing like marriage interfere with his love life, do you? Once he gets Nicole safely in hand, he'll do exactly as he pleases. Maybe that's why she'd rather come down here and play house with him occasionally than marry him. Once she actually marries Thorne, she loses her trump card, her threat that she might up and marry someone else." He paused. "And then again, maybe he really is madly in love with her and will be completely faithful. She's not exactly unattractive, you know."

"I think that plant must be a rumor mill, and you've been listening to too many of them," Juli said lightly, managing to sound much more unconcerned than she felt.

"There's another thing, too," Brian said reflectively.

He held his cup out for a coffee refill and, a little reluctantly, Juli went to the stove for the pot. She didn't like listening to Brian's suppositions and rumors, and yet there was a certain morbid fascination about hearing them.

"I doubt that Thorne really gives a damn about what people think," Brian went on. "Oh, he may give lip service to the proprieties, but he's not about to let them interfere with his life."

"I don't see what you're getting at," Juli

said cautiously, curious in spite of herself.

"It hasn't been all that long since Jason's death. If Nicole and Thorne marry too soon, it's going to be obvious they had something going while Jason was still alive. As I said, Thorne probably couldn't care less what people think, but Nicole quite likely does. Mama Taylor might even take a dim view of her former daughter-in-law marrying her son too soon."

"Surely Mrs. Taylor wouldn't put all the blame on Nicole. Thorne has to share some responsibility," Juli protested. Then she realized that she had somehow gotten into the absurd position of defending Nicole in this conversation.

"I doubt that her darling son could do anything wrong in Mama Taylor's eyes," Brian said.

Juli struggled to hold her temper and keep her expression unconcerned. It was true, of course, that Mrs. Taylor did seem quite tolerant of her son's behavior. Her easy acceptance of Juli's presence at the house Monday morning seemed to verify that. But calling that gracious, dignified woman by the sneeringly familiar term "Mama Taylor" seemed almost a sacrilege.

Neither could Juli accept what Brian was saying about Thorne's eagerness to rush

Nicole into marriage. At one time she might have believed it, but not after the lunch at his pool. To use Brian's blunt terms, Thorne obviously hadn't cared a damn about what Nicole thought or felt. He couldn't have held and kissed Juli with such passion in front of Nicole's very eyes if he did care, to say nothing of his blatant insinuations that they had spent the previous night in the same bed.

And yet, in spite of all that, there was a tiny nagging doubt way back in one corner of Juli's mind — a small, niggling suspicion that perhaps she *was* incredibly naïve, that not all was what it appeared to be in Thorne's and Nicole's sophisticated world.

"I don't know how we got off on this subject," Brian said suddenly. "I came out to see if you'd like to take in a movie. Or maybe go bowling." Seeing something negative in Juli's expression, he added hopefully, "Maybe just a drink? That wouldn't take long."

"Thanks, anyway, but I don't think so," Juli said firmly. "I'm really rather tired and it's starting to rain."

"Would you like to run up to Phoenix some weekend? It has a little more than Cholla to offer in the way of restaurants and entertainment."

"Maybe sometime," Juli said with deliberate vagueness. She stood up in what she hoped was a signal for him to go.

"I'll check with you later in the week, then," he said, evidently realizing this was not the most propitious moment to ask.

She nodded, and finally he was gone. The rain was falling quite steadily now and the air smelled fresh-washed and springy. Juli stood in the open doorway, filling her lungs with the air, determinedly discarding Brian's gossipy rumors. He meant no harm, of that she was sure, but there was something insidious about gossip and rumors. She would not leave her mind open to the damage they could do.

The rain had let up somewhat by morning, but the overcast sky was threatening more. Juli felt restless. She had done about all she could with cleaning the trailer. The weather didn't invite walking, and she didn't feel like reading. About mid-morning she decided fresh paint on the cabinets would brighten the kitchen considerably. She drove into town to pick up paint and a brush, plus a few groceries.

When she returned to the trailer, she found another of the real estate salesman's cards stuck in her door. She had somehow pushed into the back of her mind any thought that the property might sell very soon, so it was with stunned shock that she read the brief note on the back of the card. The property had just been sold. The deal was simple and straightforward: cash and no quibbling over price. He wanted her in the office that afternoon to sign some papers.

Juli dumped her sacks on the kitchen table, still stunned. She didn't want the place to sell — not now! What would she do? She couldn't just up and leave Cholla — and Thorne. The very thought made her feel dizzy and empty. Why, oh, why, did it have to sell *now!*

Unhappily, Juli glanced at her watch. It was almost noon. The salesman probably wouldn't be back in the office until later. She paced the floor. Could she turn down the offer? But that wouldn't be fair to Aunt Kate. Getting the full asking price, and in cash, was a deal that couldn't be rejected.

What would Thorne say? Would he ask her somehow to stay, perhaps even ask . . . more? Ever since Monday morning she'd had the quivery feeling that they were on the brink of something beautiful and wonderful. And now fate had seen fit to jerk the rug out from under her!

She struggled through a sandwich for lunch, hardly noticing what she ate. But by the time she headed back to town, one possible solution had occurred to her. The buyer must plan to develop the property into homesites, because that was where the value lay. And in that case the buyer was probably in no particular hurry to take possession. Just a few weeks, Juli thought tremulously, might make a lifetime of difference to her.

The real estate office was surprisingly busy when Juli walked in. The salesman waved her to a seat and said he'd be with her in a few minutes. He finally rushed over between customers and handed her some papers.

"The final papers will have to go back to your aunt for her signature, of course, but your signature on these will get things started." He handed her a pen. "You couldn't ask for a better deal. Quick and clean — no *ifs* or *ands* or other conditions. I wish we had more deals like this."

Juli took the pen hesitantly. "I hope the buyers aren't in a hurry to take possession. I'd like to . . . to stay on here a little longer."

The salesman looked surprised. "As a matter of fact, that was the one point upon which the buyer was quite insistent. Immediate possession. I was under the impression you wanted to return home as quickly as possible, so I didn't think you'd object."

"Immediate possession?" Juli echoed in dismay. "What does that mean?"

"Today, I gathered, if you could make it. But if you can get out by the end of the week, that will probably be satisfactory." He laughed. "When the Taylors want something, they don't fool around."

Juli stared at him wide-eyed. "Not . . . not the Taylors of Taylor Electronics?" she asked faintly.

"One and the same," he said cheerfully. He winked. "If I'd had any idea they might be interested, we might have upped the price a bit. But it's still a darned good deal. You won't find many buyers with all that cash."

Juli was hardly hearing. Thorne had bought the place and he wanted her out. *Now*. Why? The answer was all too obvious. He wanted to get rid of her as quickly as possible, and this was the easiest way. Juli felt dizzy with bewilderment. What had changed his mind since the lunch at his pool, when he had seemed so affectionate and kissed her so passionately? She had thought he was falling in love with her the way she had already fallen for him — and now this! With heart-stopping realization, Juli suddenly knew there had been no change in him, that his interest and affection had been nothing but a carefully calculated phony pretense.

"Miss Townsend, are you all right?" the salesman asked with concern. He reached out to steady her as she swayed.

Her mind was too numb even to fabricate an explanation for her unsteadiness. With eyes blurred with tears, she simply signed on the empty line he indicated, jammed her copies into her purse, and fled before she broke down completely.

Somehow she managed to make her way back to the car and she sat there clutching the steering wheel with unfeeling hands, grateful for the fresh downpour of rain that concealed her from passersby. Desperately, she searched for some explanation that would reveal that Thorne had purchased the property as a helpful gesture. Perhaps as a further help to Aunt Kate. That hopeful explanation was so weak that it scarcely deserved consideration, and she knew she was naïve even to consider it. Brian had been right, she thought grimly. Thorne did nothing out of pure generosity.

There was only one explanation. That earlier tenuous doubt, a suspicion so unthinkable she had refused even to acknowledge it, hit her like a blow now. He had accused her of scheming, but it was he who was the real mastermind of a calculated plan to get his own way. Juli had merely been a convenient pawn in that plan.

Not that he found her unattractive, she thought grimly, and his desire to make love to her had hardly been pretended. But that was a side issue, a momentary passion. Marrying Nicole as quickly as possible, getting her and her half of the company under his control, was his real goal, and he had seen a chance to goad her into doing what he wanted. He obviously knew Nicole well enough to realize jealousy would act as a catalyst on her, and he had cold-bloodedly used Juli to provoke Nicole's jealousy that day.

And how easily she had fallen in with his scheme, Juli thought in a flood of shame and humiliation. How willingly cooperative she had been, helping him put on a little charade for Nicole's benefit! Her face burned beneath the tears sliding across her cheeks. Thorne's game that day hadn't been to humiliate or embarrass Juli, unless that was just an added fringe benefit. Neither were his actions and words an implied apology, as she had so innocently hoped. The whole phony scene was deliberately calculated to make Nicole jealous, to show her if she didn't hurry and marry him that he might look elsewhere. It was all so plain now: the touches, the innuendos, the kiss by the gate — all cold-bloodedly calculated to arouse Nicole's jealousy. Juli herself had been aware of Nicole's jealousy that day, but she hadn't dreamed then that Thorne was deliberately baiting Nicole. Or was it just that she was too wrapped up in her own naïve dreams to see the truth?

By means fair or devious, whatever Thorne wanted, Thorne got, Juli thought bitterly, because it was obvious now that his scheme had worked. Nicole's jealousy had played into his hands, and no doubt they would soon marry. And that, of course, left Thorne with the minor but potentially messy problem of what to do about Juli now that her usefulness was over. Her love for him had been a momentary convenience, but now it was a bother to be disposed of as efficiently as possible. As usual, money seemed the most efficient means of solving the problem. He knew the sale of the property would mean her departure, and a demand for immediate possession would mean her immediate departure.

For a few reckless moments, Juli rebelled. He couldn't *force* her to leave Cholla. She could find work and get an apartment here. Brian Eames would no doubt be a willing helper.

Her defiance wilted within moments. What was the point in all that? She would only be hurting herself to stay around and watch the culmination of his skillful plan with his marriage to Nicole.

No, there was only one thing she could do. Go quietly. And as quickly as possible.

Water sheeted the windshield as Juli drove home, and her thoughts were as tumultuous and uncontrolled as the water tumbling through gullies on either side of the road. Somehow the desert seemed as un-prepared for this onslaught as Juli had been unprepared for betrayal by Thorne. The rain came too fast and heavy for the ground to absorb it. The desert cactuses looked incongruous surrounded by frothing sheets of moving water.

Closer to the trailer, however, the heavy rain seemed to be doing less damage. As the real estate salesman had once pointed out, she thought wryly, this was out of a flash-flood area.

Resolutely ignoring the weather, Juli went inside and started packing. Her own few possessions wouldn't take long to gather up, but now she had to make the final deci-sions about what things of David's she could take back to Aunt Kate in her limited car space. She tried to keep her thoughts away from Thorne, but she could no more hold them back than she could control the rain outside. Like some inescapable treadmill, her mind went over and over that glorious day hiking in the Superstitions. Her body still quivered at the memory of his passion that night and the anger and accusations that followed. Then there was the incredible surprise of the next day, when everything seemed glorious again. And now the desolate despair of knowing nothing would ever be as glorious again.

Because the despairing, almost unthinkable truth was that in spite of all that Thorne had done, she still loved him. Her, body still thrilled to the memory of his touch, the taste of his mouth, the husky chuckle of his laughter. She loved him — and he only wanted to be rid of her.

So lost was she in her unhappiness that she didn't even hear the car drive up outside. The first realization she had that anyone was near was the knock on the door. Thorne! she thought in wild jubilation. Hastily, she wiped her eyes with a tissue and raced for the door.

Brian stepped inside. He held the umbrella he was carrying outside the door to close it. Juli struggled to conceal the disappointment she knew must be written all over her face.

"Miserable weather," he muttered.

"I thought you were the guy who was tired of sunshine," Juli managed to say lightly.

He set the umbrella in a corner and took off his jacket. "I'm sure I'm not as unhappy about the rain as Thorne Taylor is." He sounded almost gleeful as he went on to tell her that the workers were just in the process of installing storm drains at the new construction site when the rains hit. The area was a mess, he said, water running everywhere. "Your friend Thorne is running everywhere, too, trying to be in three places at once," he added.

But not too busy to rush into the real estate office to buy the property and get rid of her, she thought grimly. She poured coffee and set out some date and nut candies she had bought.

"Juli, you're just going to have to get a phone," Brian grumbled. "I feel as if I'm barging in on you when I just want to talk for a minute. What are you doing?" he added suddenly, seeing the packed boxes by the sofa.

Briefly Juli explained about the sale of

the property. She didn't intend to give the name of the buyer, but Brian, ever curious, asked.

Juli struggled to make her voice neutral and casual. "Thorne Taylor. His property adjoins this. He probably wants it to keep any development from coming too close to his house."

"Oh, I see." Brian's eyes gleamed. "So that's why you've been more or less cultivating the bachelor boy. I was afraid for a while you might have some personal interest in him."

Juli tried to make some flippant reply, but the words caught in her throat. She turned away quickly, busying herself with the coffee again.

Brian looked suddenly stricken. "But that means you're leaving right away?"

"That was part of the deal, that he get immediate possession."

"I don't get it. What is his big rush?" Brian sounded half-angry, as if Thorne had deliberately interfered with *his* plans.

Juli just shrugged. She wasn't about to describe the whole humiliating, degrading experience of how Thorne had deliberately used her to make Nicole jealous and now wanted to get rid of her.

"I feel as if you're leaving before we've

hardly had a chance to get to know each other," Brian protested.

"Perhaps we can write to each other," Juli offered vaguely.

"Right. And I'm not going to be stuck here in Cholla forever. I'll be coming back East."

Juli just nodded, wishing he would go away so she could get on with her packing.

"When are you leaving?" Brian asked.

"I suppose I can get out by tomorrow. Yesterday would have suited Thorne Taylor even better," she added with a thin attempt at a smile.

"You don't have to do that," Brian said with surprising sharpness. "You don't have to jump just because *he* says so. Wait until Sunday, at least, and we'll spend all day Saturday in Phoenix. We'll eat at a good restaurant and see what else the city has to offer. We deserve that much time together."

"Oh, I don't think so," Juli demurred. "I mean, I really am supposed to be out as soon as possible."

"What's Taylor going to do if you're here a day or two extra?" Brian demanded. "Come over and toss you out bodily?"

She wouldn't put that past him, Juli thought grimly. But with the thought came a surge of rebellious defiance. Brian was right. What was Thorne going to do if she stayed a day or two longer? It might do him good to stew for a day or two, to let him wonder if she was going to make trouble. And it would certainly serve to show him he couldn't make her jump like some puppet on a string, that she would leave when she was good and ready, and not before.

"The weather could be bad," she warned. "The report is for more rain."

"That may bother Thorne Taylor sloshing around at his construction site, but we'll be snug and dry in some nice, covered shopping mall." Brian laughed.

Juli felt a stab of concern. Was the weather really damaging the new construction site? Was Thorne out in it, getting wet or cold or sick?

Of course not, she scoffed at herself. Thorne's money might not be able to stop the rain, but he could certainly hire any help he needed. He and Nicole were probably warm and cozy on that far rug in front of a crackling fire in his bedroom. The sharp clarity of that painful image in her mind lent a determination to Juli's words.

"I won't leave until Sunday," she said resolutely. "We'll spend Saturday together in Phoenix."

Chapter Ten

By Saturday morning Juli had her car almost loaded and ready to go. All that remained in the trailer were a few personal items. The weather appeared to be improving, although a rain-streaked sky just off to the north indicated that area had experienced yet another drenching downpour. Juli felt depressed and wished she had never agreed to spend this day in Phoenix with Brian.

Brian was supposed to pick her up at the trailer about nine o'clock, but by nine-thirty he still hadn't arrived. Could he have forgotten their date? she wondered. A minute later his car pulled into the driveway and she realized the reason for his delay. The right fender of the car was crumpled, the hood dented, and the door scratched. He slammed out of the car and stalked toward the trailer after a surly glance at his damaged car.

She opened the trailer door. "What happened?" she exclaimed. "Are you all right?"

"Some idiot pulled out of a parking

space and smashed into me!" he snarled. "Outside of being ready to commit murder, I suppose I'm all right. I hope you're ready," he added, as if her not being ready would be the last straw. He didn't seem to notice that she was wearing a feminine, full-skirted mint-green dress and high heels because she knew he preferred dresses to pants.

It was hardly an auspicious beginning for a day about which Juli was already unenthusiastic. "Perhaps we ought to call today off," Juli suggested. "You can't enjoy yourself after what happened to your car. And the radio said there's been some minor flooding in Phoenix because they had to release water from above one of the Salt River Project dams."

"We're going. If there's one thing I am going to do, it's get out of Cholla for a day," Brian muttered grimly.

Concealing a sigh, Juli picked up her purse and they got into the car. The crumpled fender had an irritating rattle that Juli suspected would drive her crazy before the day was over, but Brian just scowled and drove on. They were about halfway to town when a pickup traveling at high speed approached them.

"Idiot driver!" Brian growled, though

the pickup didn't come anywhere near them.

Juli involuntarily clutched the door handle as the pickup whizzed by. Brian evidently hadn't noticed what Juli had — that the pickup was Thorne's four-wheel-drive vehicle, and Thorne was driving. He must be going out to the trailer. Why? To inspect his newly purchased property and make sure she was gone, no doubt. He was in for a surprise, then, she thought with a certain grim satisfaction, thinking of her car still parked squarely in the yard. She was uncertain whether or not he had recognized Brian's car or seen her in it. She was relieved she had gotten away from the trailer before he arrived and created some unpleasant scene.

Brian surprised her by taking the old road that cut across the dry riverbed to join the newer highway farther north. It was a paved road, but rough and potholed, and he had always seemed too fussy about his car to drive on such a road. She was further surprised to see the riverbed was no longer dry, that a wide expanse of water now covered the roadway. A pickup was pulling out on the far side, evidently having just forded the water.

Brian braked, scowled, then started forward toward the point where the paved road disappeared into the flowing water.

"What are you going to do?" Juli gasped.

"Drive across to the other side."

"But is it safe?" Juli questioned doubtfully. "The water seems to be moving rather fast."

"The pickup just crossed here."

"But it was a much larger vehicle," Juli pointed out. "The water will come up much farther on this car. Perhaps we should go around by the bridge."

"No, I am not going to drive all the way around by the bridge," Brian snapped. The front tires were touching the water now.

Juli tried a different tack. "But the water looks terribly muddy. Won't it ruin the paint on your car?"

It was the wrong thing to say.

"The water can't be more than a few inches deep, and it can't damage the car a damned bit more than it already is," Brian said sourly, eyeing the dented hood.

He acted, Juli thought in exasperation, almost as if the car were to blame for getting damaged and he was out to punish it still further. With him in this unpleasant mood, she thoroughly wished she had refused to come along. Stubbornly, he drove forward, and the water gurgled and sucked at the underside of the car.

"It's deeper than it looks," he muttered. "Why the hell don't they build roads with bridges in this country like they do everywhere else?"

"The riverbed is dry about ninety-nine percent of the time. Maybe they figure people will have enough sense to go around by the bridge when there's water in the riverbed," Juli retorted. Her annoyance at Brian's stubbornness was changing to alarm. The far side of the road still looked a long distance away, and the water wasn't getting any more shallow.

"Look, what's that?" Juli cried, pointing to some branches caught in the roadway ahead of them, a few straggly leaves showing above the water to mark a tangle beneath.

"Damn!" Brian muttered. He jerked the steering wheel to the right to avoid the branches, and then suddenly the car sagged and tilted to one side. In horror Juli saw water rising through the floorboards.

"What happened?" she cried.

Brian exploded with another oath. "The wheels on that side must have gone off the pavement!"

Juli was sitting at an angle on the tilted seat. She lifted her feet to keep them out of the water seeping in. Brian gunned the engine and the car jolted forward, only to tilt even farther. Then the engine sputtered and died.

"The engine must be wet," he muttered. He turned the key and pumped the accelerator, but the engine only coughed and sputtered uselessly.

"Look!" Juli cried. A road-maintenance truck had pulled up on the far side of the river and the crew was placing barricades across the pavement. One man was shouting and waving his arms at them.

Brian, on the high side of the car, opened his window and managed to lean out. When he looked back at Juli, his face had visibly paled. "He says there was a cloudburst north of here and another foot of water may come through here within the next half-hour. I guess we'd better wade to shore."

He opened the door and, grimacing in distaste, stepped out. Juli scrambled across the bucket seats, then hesitated when she saw the muddy water swirling around Brian's legs.

"Come on! I think it's already rising!"

Gingerly, Juli stepped into the water and felt the current pushing against her legs, threatening to unbalance her as she wobbled in her high-heeled sandals. Swiftly, she kicked off her high heels. Together they worked their way around the car. Juli was dismayed to see how far they had driven. They were almost in the middle of the riverbed.

"If I get out of this, I am leaving this miserable place and never coming back!" Brian muttered.

Juli didn't bother to reply, thinking that if it weren't for his stubbornness and anger, they wouldn't even be in this predicament. She felt her way forward in her bare feet, her full skirt floating around her. Brian kept a hand on her elbow, but when he muttered something about not being able to swim, Juli suspected he was clinging to her more for safety rather than to assist her.

A mesquite branch floated by, jabbing Juli with sharp thorns. The water sucked and pulled greedily at her legs. Once she stepped into a pothole and almost fell. Finally, the pavement beneath their feet slanted upward and the water became more shallow. Juli was in water below her knees when it happened. She stepped on something sharp with a bare foot, jerked back, stumbled, and crashed into the swirling water. Somehow in the process she tripped Brian and he fell across her. Juli came up sputtering and wiping her eyes and trying to get out from under Brian's wet weight.

"Well, are you two enjoying yourselves?"

Juli scrambled to her feet at the sound of the caustic voice. Thorne, hands on lean hips, stood beside his big pickup at the edge of the water.

"What do you mean, pulling a stupid stunt like this?" he demanded, his gaze flicking across both of them and then to the stranded car.

"Good heavens, we're drowning and my car is washing away and he decides to cross-examine us!" Brian muttered.

Juli didn't bother to answer either of the men. She was coldly furious with both — Brian for attempting what really was a stupid thing to do; Thorne for standing there looking at them both with such contemptuous superiority. With as much dignity as possible, considering her bedraggled clothing and disheveled condition, Juli held her head high and started toward the dry bank, only to stumble into another pothole and tumble headlong into the water again.

She was out of danger now and the fall didn't really hurt, but tears of frustration and humiliation sprang to Juli's eyes. That

Thorne should see her like this, hair straggly, dress limp and dirty, pantyhose in tatters around her feet, was almost more than she could bear. But she wouldn't let him see how humiliated she felt. She wouldn't! She floundered to her feet, surprised to find how the struggle to reach shore had weakened her. Then two strong arms lifted her from the water and carried her to the pickup. Thorne thrust her inside, took off his jacket, and wrapped it roughly around her.

"You stay here," he commanded brusquely.

Juli was too limp and weak to protest and only nodded numbly. By now Brian was out of the water, too, looking as bedraggled as she felt. There was a helpless look on his face as he stared at his car. Juli shivered. The water looked higher now than when they had crawled out of the car.

Without a glance at Brian, Thorne pulled a cable out of the winch attached to the front of the pickup and started toward the car, ignoring the water rushing by and fending off branches and debris swirling around him. Juli watched with a frightened fascination as he reached beneath the dirty water to attach the hook to the car. Brian paced along the edge of the water. Thorne made his way back to the pickup, holding onto the cable as the increasing strength of the current tried to drag him away.

Back at the pickup, Thorne activated the winch and slowly inched the car backward through the water. Then he moved the pickup, dragging the smaller car with it to higher ground in case the water rose still farther. He got out of the pickup, detached the cable from the car, and rewound it on the winch. It was all done so efficiently that Juli was left marveling in spite of her anger at his disdainful attitude. Brian mumbled his thanks, which Thorne ignored, except to say curtly that he would send a tow truck for the car.

No mention was made of Juli in the conversation, and Brian offered no objections as Thorne prepared to drive off with her in the pickup. A road crew arrived and Thorne opened the window and talked to them a moment. They said they were late in barricading this road because several subdivision streets had flooded, endangering homes. When Juli glanced back as the pickup drove away, Brian was examining the car, evidently more worried about it than Juli.

Thorne switched on the heater, sending a warm blast of air into the pickup cab. At a service station he stopped and telephoned for a tow truck. He seemed oblivious to his wet boots and pants, but Juli couldn't seem to stop shivering. When he returned he gave Juli a long, appraising look and finally spoke to her.

"Where on earth were you and Eames going?"

"To Phoenix."

"For what reason?"

"To . . . to celebrate my leaving!" she said defiantly. She might be soaked and shivering, but she refused to be humble.

"That was a damned stupid thing Eames did, trying to cross the water like that!" he growled.

"I believe you've already mentioned that once," Juli said, her voice aloof and distant. They drove along in a rather tense silence until Juli realized they were not on the road that led to the trailer.

"Where are you taking me?" she demanded.

"To my place."

"What do you mean by that? They're *both* your places now," she retorted pointedly.

He glanced over at her, forehead creased in a scowl that was half-angry, half-puzzled. She saw with an unexpected pang that a branch or the cable had grazed his jaw, leaving a raw, scraped area. She looked away. She didn't want to be touched by any concern for him.

"And what do *you* mean?" he demanded.

"You don't have to explain," Juli said. She had finally stopped shivering and she let the jacket slip away from her shoulders. Then, as Thorne glanced at her again and she realized the wet material clung to her breasts like a second skin, she hastily replaced the jacket.

He clenched his jaw, as if annoyed by the temporary distraction, and then said angrily, "Dammit, there isn't anything to explain! I'm not responsible for Nicole's underhanded schemes!"

"Nicole's schemes!" Juli repeated scathingly. "You deliberately used me to make Nicole jealous enough to marry you right away. Then you bought the trailer and property to get rid of me as fast as possible."

"Where did you ever get such a crazy, mixed-up idea like that?" he asked, his voice incredulous. "You really think *I* bought the place?"

"You don't need to raise your voice like that just because I figured out your little scheme," Juli said frostily. "It worked. I'm leaving in the morning."

"I will use any tone of voice I want when you come up with some fool story like that," he said grimly. "Nicole bought the property. I didn't know anything about it until a couple of hours ago. I've been working around the clock at the plant trying to save the construction site. If I hadn't, it could have been wiped out."

"Nicole bought the property?" Juli faltered.

"Yes, Nicole bought the property," he repeated in exasperation. "You must have signed the papers agreeing to the sale. Didn't you *read* them?"

No, Juli realized, she hadn't read them. She fumbled in the seat for her purse. The outside of the purse was wet from the spills she had taken, but the inside was relatively dry. She found the papers where she had stuffed them unread in the bottom of the purse. With a mixed sense of bewilderment and wonder, she realized he was right. Nicole Taylor was the purchaser. She replaced the papers in her purse, stubbornly refusing to let him know that she hadn't read the papers because her eyes had been too blinded with tears at the thought of what he had done.

"So Nicole bought the property," Juli

finally said. "I'm sure that worked in nicely with your plans."

He exploded. "Juli, if you don't stop —"

"Very well, then, tell me *why* Nicole bought the property," she challenged.

"I'm sure I can't begin to explain the workings of Nicole's devious little mind," Thorne snapped. He hesitated, then said in a different voice, "Perhaps she did it because . . . because she thought I was falling in love with you."

Juli's heart lurched, but somehow she managed to keep her voice cold and aloof. "A natural mistake, I'm sure," she agreed, "after the charade you played for her benefit at lunch the other day." She didn't intend to say more, but in remembered outrage the words spilled out. "Insinuating we spent the night together. And —"

"The fact that we didn't wasn't for my lack of effort," he commented dryly.

Juli ignored that. "Kissing me like that right in front of her, so she had to see! It was humiliating!"

"Oh? Humiliating to whom? *You* seemed to be enjoying the kiss."

"That was before I realized how you were deliberately using me to make Nicole jealous," Juli repeated.

"Juli, I'm warning you —" he began angrily. Then he clamped his jaw shut. "We'll discuss this later. I think the water has muddled your head."

He drove under the archway to the estate and parked in front of the house. He pulled Juli roughly across the pickup seat, tossing the jacket aside. She was embarrassed at the way the wet material clung to her breasts and wrapped itself around her thighs. She also realized that the filmy mint-green material when wet was practically transparent. If she thought he would ignore that, she was wrong. He eyed her appraisingly.

"You ought to sue the dressmaker for indecently exposing you." He swept her up in his arms and started toward the house. "Or perhaps you'd rather make a million posing for some poster shots. That outfit beats a wet T-shirt any day."

Juli refused to dignify the remarks with a retort of her own. She folded her arms across her breasts and held her body as distantly rigid as possible under the circumstances. She knew better than to try to fight against him, knew resistance to his greater strength and determination was useless. He carried her inside and down the hall and plopped her at the bathroom door.

"You can clean up in there," he stated. "Hand your clothes out to me and I'll have Estelle take care of them. I'll bring you something else to wear."

Juli hesitated, rebellious against the way he threw out commands, but reluctantly realizing she couldn't just stand there dripping puddles all over the floor.

"I'll only be a few minutes, and then I want to go home — to the trailer, I mean," she amended, remembering it was Nicole's property now.

She stepped inside and closed the door. She unzipped the wet dress and stepped out of it. Concealing herself carefully behind the door, she reached around it and handed the dress to Thorne.

"I said I wanted your clothes," he growled. "All your clothes."

"I have no intention of giving you —"

"All your clothes," he repeated.

Angrily, she slammed the door shut again and a moment later handed out her lacy underthings, feeling her face flame and only glad he couldn't see that, as well as her most private items of clothing. Why, oh, why, had she chosen today to wear the almost wickedly lacy underthings? She eyed herself in the gleaming expanse of mirror, the pattern of tan and white skin covering her like some indecently reversed article of clothing. Hurriedly, she turned on the shower knobs and washed away the grimy remains of her bout with the river water. It seemed, she thought with exasperation, that she was always arriving here in something less than her most presentable condition. She was toweling herself dry when there was a knock on the door.

"Open the door. I'll give you something to put on."

"You could have sent Estelle," she snapped.

"Yes, I could have," he agreed. "But I didn't."

Keeping a towel draped around her, she opened the door and stuck her hand out. She pulled back a man's royal-blue dressing gown, several sizes too large, but silky feeling against her bare skin. She determinedly fought down an odd little rush of excitement at the realization that she was wearing such a personal item of Thorne's clothing.

"Thank you," she said coolly. "Please let me know when my own clothes are ready." She sat down on the padded stool in front of the dressing table and prepared to wait.

"I'd like to talk to you," he said.

Juli didn't reply.

"I said I'd like to talk to you," he repeated more loudly. When she still didn't reply, he added grimly, "Either you come out here and talk to me, or I'm coming in there and talk to you."

In panic she heard something brush against the door, as if he might be testing his shoulder on it, and she had no doubt that if she delayed too long he just might break the door down.

"I'm coming out," she said, trying not to sound shaky. She checked to make sure the oversized robe covered her thoroughly and tightened the rope belt around her waist. She opened the door and stared up at him defiantly. He had changed to dry clothes.

"Well, what did you want to discuss?" she demanded. A dismaying thought occurred to her. "Where is Nicole?"

"On her way to Scottsdale, I presume. We'll go to the den," he said decisively.

He followed her down the hall. Juli was uncomfortably aware that the silky robe, though oversized, was not exactly unrevealing in the way it clung to her derrière. She was glad when they reached the den and she could sit down.

"Where is your mother?" Juli asked uneasily.

"Shopping. But don't worry. You don't

need a chaperone. I'm not going to behave the way I did the other night."

That was good, Juli thought, because she was feeling strangely light-headed, remembering with tingling warmth that other night in this very room.

"Now, about the property," he began.

"If Nicole bought the place and not you, why did you go out there this morning?" she demanded.

"I was afraid you had already picked up and left while I was involved with problems at the plant."

"Evidently, your little scheme to make Nicole jealous was even more effective than you planned," Juli commented. "She was jealous enough to spend a good chunk of money to get me out of the way."

"That is at least twice now that you have accused me of deliberately making Nicole jealous," he said angrily.

"Are you denying it?" she challenged.

"Yes. I certainly am denying it!" he said hotly. "I wasn't trying to make her jealous. I simply wanted to make plain to Nicole once and for all that I am *not* in love with her and I am *not* going to marry her."

Juli's heart thundered at the vehement words and she clutched the robe belt to control the trembling of her hands. "But everyone says . . . I mean, everyone knows you and she —"

"She and I *what?*"

"That you were in love with her before she married your brother. That you played around together even after they were married. That you were just waiting for a respectable interval of time to pass before marrying her now. That you *had* to marry her to keep control of the company!"

"I don't have to do anything," he retorted. "And I certainly don't have to marry Nicole. Jason and I had already made the necessary legal arrangements so that if anything happened to one of us, the surviving brother inherited a small portion of the other's holdings — enough to retain control of the company. And even if that weren't true, I wouldn't marry some woman I didn't love just for the sake of the company!"

Juli was beginning to feel something soft and eager opening within her with each word he spoke. The words almost sang around her. He wasn't in love with Nicole and he had no intention of marrying her for any reason. "But you were in love with her once?" she persisted, still hardly able to believe what she was hearing.

He scowled. He went over to a cabinet

and poured a drink. She shook her head when he raised the glass, offering her one. "Yes and no. Once, a long time ago, I thought I was in love with Nicole. But I quickly woke up when I recognized her scheming, devious ways."

"You considered her throwing you over to marry Jason 'devious'?" Juli couldn't keep the doubt out of her mind or voice. "She couldn't help herself if she just fell in love with him."

"Everyone thought that was the way it happened." There was a long, taut silence while he looked broodingly at the drink, "That was what I wanted everyone to think."

"Why?"

"For Jason's sake. So he wouldn't know she married him mostly for spite when I told her I wouldn't marry her."

"Oh!" The soft exclamation slipped between Juli's lips as she realized what Thorne had done to protect his brother's feelings. Everything was so different from what she had thought, and now she was seeing in Thorne again one of the traits that had made her tumble headlong in love with him. So much in love that even when she doubted him and was in painful torment, her love had never vanished. It surged back now, stronger than ever. But still she had to ask, "And the rumors about Nicole and you seeing each other after she and Jason were married?"

He shook his head and his mouth twisted in a bitter smile. "I don't know, unless people just enjoy passing around juicy gossip without regard to its accuracy."

"Why didn't she and Jason live here instead of Scottsdale?"

"Unfortunately, Jason heard the rumors, too, and I'm afraid he never fully believed it was over between us." Thorne's regretful voice hardened. "But it was."

Juli paused, breath held, wishing she could let it go right there. But she couldn't. She had to ask. "It was over — until he died."

Thorne looked up sharply, eyes narrowing. "I made the mistake of trying to be kind and helpful to Nicole after Jason's death. I did it for Jason, because he loved her. But she misunderstood my motives. That was why I finally had to pull that little scene in front of her the other morning. It was the only way to make her see the light. And I'm not sure even that convinced her. Some women manage to see only what they want to see."

His words hung in the air as he scowled

into the liquid amber of his drink, and the soft warmth that had flowered within Juli suddenly shriveled in a cold chill. *Some women manage to see only what they want to see.* She had done it again, she realized in despair. What a naïve fool she was! Thorne wasn't in love with Nicole; that was obvious now. But she had just now naïvely interpreted that to mean he must have feelings for *her*, and that wasn't true at all! The reasons for his playing out that little scene in front of Nicole were different from what she had assumed, but that didn't change the fact that it was all just a charade played out for Nicole's benefit. He had coldbloodedly played with Juli's heart for his own purposes. His display of affection had been merely an act to rid himself of the unwanted attentions of another woman.

Juli stood up. "So now you're rid of Nicole. Congratulations. But she still owns the property, and I'm supposed to be out this weekend. So if I could trouble you to take me home now — ?" Juli didn't look at Thorne, afraid he might see the bright glitter of tears in her eyes. "You'll stay at the trailer as long as you want," he said. There was a determined thrust to his jaw. "Don't worry about Nicole. I'll take care of her."

What was that for? Juli thought bitterly. A reward for playing her part satisfactorily in the little scene for Nicole's benefit? "I want to leave as soon as possible. Please take me back to the trailer."

"No. You're not going anywhere just yet."

"We've been through this before, but this time you're not stopping me! If you're too busy to take me, I'll just call a cab and go."

"Like that?" he questioned, his tilted eyebrows jeering at her attire.

Juli paused on her way to the desk phone. She had no idea where her clothes were, and it was doubtful if they were dry yet, anyway. "Yes, like this, if I have to," she retorted defiantly.

"Oh, no, you're not," he said grimly. "If you're walking out of here, it's not going to be wearing *my* bathrobe."

With surprising swiftness, he reached out and jerked loose the rope cord around her waist. She clutched frantically at the silky material, wrapping it around her and holding it with both hands. With both his hands he grabbed the front of the robe, ready to use full force to rip it away from her.

"You wouldn't!" she gasped furiously.

"I would." His hands didn't loosen. "So

if you'd care to greet your cabbie naked, just go ahead and make your call."

She jerked away from him, knowing he was fully capable of carrying out his threat to leave her standing there helplessly naked.

"Very well, but I . . . I'm leaving as soon as my clothes are dry."

He released his hands warily and turned back to his drink. "You're being quite stubborn and unreasonable —"

"I'm being unreasonable!" she gasped. "How about *your* ridiculous and totally unreasonable accusation that I deliberately schemed to get in bed with you?"

He had the decency to flush slightly. "I'm sorry about that. I was . . ." He hesitated, then finished slowly: "I guess I was disappointed. I thought you were different, and then it appeared that you were as scheming and devious as Nicole."

"So, if you believed that, and you evidently believed it before we left the trailer that night, why did you bring me here? Why didn't you just walk off and leave me?"

He scowled. "Because I couldn't. Because I wanted you even if you were scheming."

"And so you behaved like a . . . a savage! Throwing me into a bedroom and practically holding me captive, just like you're doing now." Juli's lips compressed as she blinked back tears, because she knew that in spite of all that had happened, it was more than her body that was captive here. It was her heart. And though her body might soon be released, her heart would never be free because she loved him still.

"I know I behaved . . . badly," he growled in reluctant admission. "But you made me furious and frustrated. I didn't want to want you — but I did. I didn't want to be in love with you, but I was. I am in love with you. . . ." He spoke the words with an odd helplessness, as if they were unfamiliar and beyond his usual iron self-control.

They were staring at each other, Juli's eyes wide with wonder, when Estelle tapped on the doorframe and then peered inside.

"Your clothes are ready."

"Thank you," Juli said. Estelle came in and handed Juli the dress on a hanger. She placed the other items, discreetly folded into a neat bundle, on the coffee table. When Estelle was gone, Thorne looked at Juli.

"So, you have your clothes. You're free now," he said. "I can't hold you captive if you want to go."

"Are you asking me to stay — longer?"

Her eyes, dark with emotion, lifted to meet his again.

He took one long stride toward her and flung the dress toward the sofa with a rough gesture. "I'm asking you to stay for today — tomorrow — forever! As my wife," he finished huskily.

Juli's hands left the folds of the silky robe and crept toward his neck, heedless of the way the silky material of the robe threatened to slither open. With hands that had an uncharacteristic tremble, Thorne removed her arms from around his neck and placed them in control of the robe again.

"You'd better keep yourself covered, or —"

"Or what?" Juli's eyes danced.

"I might not be able to live up to my promise not to behave the way I did the other night. And you'd better not wait too long to set the date for our wedding day," he warned.

"I was under the impression you made all the important decisions," Juli teased.

The light in his eyes suddenly changed. "Sometimes I try to. But there's one decision I can't make, because you have to make it. I'm talking about our getting married, but you've never said yes — or no —"

Juli lifted her mouth to his, but he stopped her.

"No, you have to say it!" he demanded imperiously.

"I love you. I want to marry you."

He smiled, satisfied, and his arms closed around her, capturing her, as her heart was already his captive forever.